I0831277

Hayward's Unabridged Dictionary

The second volume in
a collection of writings by

C.J.S. Hayward

C.J.S. Hayward Publications, Wheaton

1. Christianity. 2. Social commentary. 3. Satire. 4. Web Design. 5. Computer Programming--Java. 6. Spam. 7. Christianity--koans. 8. Business. 9. Mathematics. 10. Dictionaries--satirical.

ISBN 978-0-6151-9362-5

The reader is invited to visit CJSHayward.com.

Contents

An Open Letter to Spam Patrons

Dear Valued Patron;

How would you like to associate your organization with false advertising, illegal marketing scams, snake oil diets, and unsolicited pornography? You can--it's easier than you think. You can reach thousands of people for every penny you invest. The only real cost is to your reputation.

What? That doesn't sound attractive to you? Too bad. You're doing all that--and more--every single time you send unsolicited bulk e-mail. It's also known as *spam*, and for good reason. Why?

In a classic Monty Python sketch, a customer in a restaurant asks what's on the menu. The waitress tells him, "Well, there's egg and bacon; egg, sausage, and bacon; egg and spam; egg, bacon, and spam; egg, bacon, sausage, spam; spam, bacon, sausage, and spam; spam, egg, spam, spam, bacon, and spam; spam, sausage, spam, spam, spam, bacon, spam, tomato, and spam; spam, spam, spam, egg, and spam" (and so on). Then a chorus of Vikings begins chanting, "Spam, spam, spam, spam; lovely spam, wonderful spam." The waitress just doesn't get it, even when the customer repeats that he *doesn't like spam*.

You may be the victim of false advertising. Many spammers advertise "opt-in e-mail lists" with millions of targeted recipients--but please think for a moment. Would *you* choose to be on a mailing list that let advertisers fill your mailbox dirt-cheap? Are there millions of people who would choose to have a mailbox with advertisement, advertisement, personal letter, advertisement, family newsletter, and *your* advertisement? If someone has asked you to read this page, there's a good chance you've patronized spam--and been advertised along with snake oil diets and illegal marketing scams. Don't you think you're in bad company?

You don't have to be. If you want more information, you can read Stopping Spam: Stamping Out Unwanted E-mail and News Postings. It's one of O'Reilly & Associates' best-selling titles. But, most importantly, you can *stop paying people to make you look bad*. Think about it.

Sincerely,
C.J.S. Hayward
CJSHayward.com

All I Really Needed to Learn about Programming, I Learned from Java

```
Write once, debug everywhere();
Prefer compile time errors to run time
    errors();
Gotos and pointers are like bad words --
    they can get you into a lot of
    trouble();
Novice-friendliness and expert-friendliness
    are at a trade-off();
An intentionally simple syntax is compatible
    with a complex collection of objects();
Programming in a high level language is
    faster than programming in a lower level
    language();
It takes longer to learn the high level ways
    of calling algorithms than the low level
    building blocks needed to implement
    them();
Every once in a while, you will be surprised
    at what you have to implement yourself
    -- a ready-made method to return a
    stacktrace as a string, or have a method
    find its caller's class();
```

```
Use the most restrictive keywords you can --
    it's kindness in disguise();
If you want to circumvent security, you
    can't cast to (char *) and reconstruct
    private members();
If you want to circumvent security, you very
    well may be able to serialize to a
    stream and reconstruct private
    members();
Resurrect objects and die(); There are some
    things that words cannot explain -- for
    everything else, there are over 100 megs
    of documentation();
Your program will see much more use if
    people can run it from their browsers();
You can program your server to use any
    encryption algorithm allowed, but you
    can't stop your clients from storing
    their private keys on unsecured Windows
    boxes();
Carefully designed languages can reduce
    bugs, but debugging will always be a
    part of programming();
No matter how carefully designed the
    language is, people will still write
    code that should be indented six feet
    downwards and covered with dirt();
A good new language makes it unnecessary to
    use older ones, just as a good cordless
    screwdriver makes it unnecessary to use
    a hammer or a wrench();
You can lead a programmer to objects, but
    you can't make him think();
You can paint on a glass pane in your
    computer or at your house -- but just
    because you are allowed to do it doesn't
    mean it's (usually) a good idea();
```

```
Writing a DWIM compiler is AI-complete();
No matter how fast computers get, there will
    always be a way to make them move like
    molasses();
There wMemory fault. Core dumped.
```

The Modern Baccalaureate

Baccalaureate:
I am the very model of a modern baccalaureate;
I know of data structures, algorithms, a-and languages;
I know of the-ory's giants, and I quote programming idioms,
From foo or die to for loop, arrang-ed by a radix sort;
I'm very well acquainted, too, with matters theoretical,
I know many algorithms, both the simple and quadratical,
About exponential time I'm teeming with lots o' news,
With many cheerful facts about the problems intractaloose.
Chorus:
With many cheerful facts about the problems intractaloose.
With many cheerful facts about the problems intractaloose.
With many cheerful facts about the problems intractatractaloose.
Baccalaureate:
I'm very good at top-down and bottom-up appro-o-oaches;
I know the technific terms for things very numerous:
In short, in data structures, algorithms, and languages,
I am the very model of a modern baccalaureate.
Chorus:
In short, in data structures, algorithms, and languages,
He is the very model of a modern baccalaureate.
Baccalaureate:
I know the classic games, from ro-o-ogue to moria;

I answer challenge problems; I've a pretty taste for recursia;
I quote, in great detail, all the flaws of frightful Windows;
In tuning I can bring speedups incredibles;
        I can tell classic code from tha-at of a fre-eshman
I know the tables ASCII and EBCDIC in base 10!
Then I can tell a joke of which I've heard the theme afore,
And recite all the words from the UL spam recipe!
        Chorus:
And recite all the words from the UL spam recipe!
And recite all the words from the UL spam recipe!
And recite all the words from the UL spam recirecipe!
        Baccalaureate:
Then I can write a rot-13 in x86 assembler,
And tell you how to list a set's every member,
In short, in data structures, algorithms, and languages,
I am the very model of a modern baccalaureate.
        Chorus:
In short, in data structures, algorithms, and languages,
I am the very model of a modern baccalaureate.
        Baccalaureate:
(Slowly)
In fact, when I know what is meant by "person" and "humanities",
When I can tell at sight if someone's a smi-ilin' or a weepin',
When such affairs as songs and friendship I kno-ow of,
And when I know precisely what is meant by "sociology",
        When I guess what depth hides in real community,
When I know more of French than a young boy watching tele-
vee--
In short, when I've a smattering of thoughts from the humanities--
(Vivace)
You'll say a better baccalaureate has never sat a gees--
        Chorus:
You'll say a better baccalaureate has never sat a gees,
You'll say a better baccalaureate has never sat a gees,
You'll say a better baccalaureate has never sat a sat a gees,
        Baccalaureate:

For my liberal arts knowledge, tho' I'm clever and intelligent,
Fails to include many things the most magnificent;
But still, in data structures, algorithms, and languages,
I am the very model of a modern baccalaureate.

Chorus:

But still, in data structures, algorithms, and languages,
He is the very model of a modern baccalaureate.

The Case for Uncreative Web Design

When the Master governs, people are hardly aware that he exists.
Next best is a leader who is loved.
Next, one who is feared.
The worst is one who is despised.
Lao Tze, *Tao Te Ching*, tr. Stephen Mitchell

In looking at various award review sites, I have seen people equating creative web design with good web design. This is not simply in acknowledgement that creativity is one of the gifts of the human mind and an indispensable part of the great triumphs of human culture. It goes further to take the perspective that "good web design" means design that impresses the viewer with its creativity. This perspective, which is almost never questioned among awards reviewers, is one which is eminently worthy of question.

Good acting does not leave people impressed with how good the acting is. The very best acting leads people to be so involved with the drama and tension that they forget they are watching actors at all. Not all acting reaches that standard -- which is a very high standard -- but acting has the quality that, at its best, it is *transparent*: people see through the acting to the important thing, the story.

What are the basic responses to my A Dream of Light? In order from best to worst:

- Best: The reader is moved by the images and stimulated by the ideas, and leaves the reading a wiser person. Perhaps this involves being impressed by the thoughts, but the reader who is impressed is impressed as a side effect of the literature's power. The reader leaves the reading thinking about the writing's subject-matter.
- Second best: The reader's primary response is to think about how smart I am, or how eccentric, or something of that sort. The writing has not completely succeeded. The reader leaves the reading thinking about me.
- Worst: The reader reads it and walks away thinking about the page's design, even how clean and uncluttered it is. The reader leaves the reading thinking about the web design.

If a reader walks away from that piece of literature thinking about my web design, the design is a failure. The design is as bad as a photograph where the scene is blocked by the photographer's thumb.

It is sometimes easy for webmasters to forget that readers spend most of their time viewing other pages -- not figuring out mine. I intentionally employ a standard web design in nearly all of my pages: navigation bar to the left, and a body to the right with dark text on a light background, different colors for *visited* and *unvisited* links (with *visited* links looking washed-out compared to *unvisited* links), no frames, judicious use of *emphasized text*, a header at the top, and navigation links at the bottom. I do not use any technology just because it's there -- one page uses Java, and has content that would be almost meaningless if the applet were not there. The design on my home page is not creative, because it is intended *not* to be creative. I copied best practices from other sites and from friends' suggestions, in order to make a design that gets out of the way so readers can see the content.

To adapt a classic proverb: *Don't bother to impress people with creative design when you can impress people with creative content*. My web design is not evidence of any great creativity, but many readers have found the content in my writings to show considerable creativity. I employ a very standardized web design for the same reason that I use standard spellings and grammar when I write: I want people to be able to see through them to whatever it is I'm writing about. Yf spelynge caulze uttinshun too ihtselv, itt yss mahch herdyr too thynque abaut whutt iz beeynge sayde. If, on the other hand, people employ standard spellings, readers can ignore the spelling and focus on the point the writer is trying to make. The spelling is *transparent*. Spelling is not where you want to demonstrate your creativity. And neither, usually, is web design.

Now, does that mean there is no place for creativity in design? No! In I learned it all from Jesus, I had each sentence a different color from the one before, and none of it black -- which I regard as a legitimate artistic liberty. The Quintessential Web Page is aiming at a quite different effect (humorous rather than artistic), and it does other things that are not ordinarily appropriate. In this page, I use the content to draw attention to the design -- also not normally appropriate. These things are not a special privilege for me; I just mention my pages because they're the ones I know best. There's some really beautiful Flash art on the web. One human-computer interaction expert has created a usability resource that is one of the ugliest pages I have ever seen, and does almost every major no-no on the list. This is as it should be -- he is making a point by demonstrating features of bad web design. In that regard, making a page that is singularly annoying makes the point far more forcefully than an exemplar of good web practices that says "Be careful that you don't have text that's indistinguishable from your background." It is perfectly acceptable to stray from general rules *if* you have strong and specific reason to violate them. I learned it all from Jesus, in my opinion, is a unique and valuable addition to my web page -- but if I made every page look like that, my PageRank would drop through the floor.

Picasso said, "Good artists copy. Great artists steal." Great artists never believe they have to invent everything from scratch to make good art -- instead, they draw on the best that has been done before, and use their own creativity to *build on top of what others have already accomplished*. In web design, this means making a site that is usable to viewers who have learned how to use other sites.

A careful reader will notice one element of design on this site that is not standard, but should be. Designers for major sites, who often have excellent vision, will put navigation links on the page, but make them as small as they can be and not be completely illegible. This is a truly bad idea, and I don't understand why it is so common. (Maybe web designers forget that some of us only have 20/20 vision?) The navigation links are some of the most important links on most web pages, and I wish to say, "Yes! I consider these links important for you to be able to read and use, and I will proudly let you read them at whatever your preferred text size is, *not* the smallest size I can read!"

I will consider this to be a successful design feature if visitors normally don't notice it unless someone points it out.

The Administrator who Cried, "Important!"

Once upon a time, there was a new employee, hired fresh out of college by a big company. The first day on the job, he attended a pep rally, filled out paperwork concerning taxes and insurance, and received a two page document that said at the top, "Sexual Harassment Policy: Important. Read Very Carefully!"

So our employee read the sexual harassment policy with utmost care, and signed at the bottom indicating that he had read it. The policy was a remedial course in common sense, although parts of it showed a decided lack of common sense. It was an insult to both his intelligence and his social maturity.

Our employee was slightly puzzled as to why he was expected to read such a document that carefully, but soon pushed doubts out of his mind. He trotted over to his new cubicle, sat down, and began to read the two inch thick manual on core essentials that every employee needs to know. He was still reading core essentials two hours later when his boss came by and said, "Could you take a break from that? I want to introduce you to your new co-workers, and show you around."

So our employee talked with his boss -- a knowledgeable, competent, and understanding woman -- and enjoyed meeting his co-workers, trying to learn their names. He didn't have very much other work yet, so he dutifully read everything that the administrators sent him -- even the ones that didn't say "Important -- please read" at the top. He read about ISO 9001 certification, continual changes and updates to company policy, new technologies that the company was adopting, employee discounts, customer success stories, and other oddments totalling to at least a quarter inch of paper each day, not counting e-mails.

His boss saw that he worked well, and began to assign more difficult tasks appropriate to his talent. He took on this new workload while continuing to read everything the administration told him to read, and worked longer and longer days.

One day, a veteran came and put a hand on his shoulder, saying, "Kid, just between the two of us, you don't have to read every piece of paper that says 'Important' at the top. None of us read all that."

And so our friend began to glance at the first pages of long memos, to see if they said anything helpful for him to know, and found that most of them did not. Some time after that, he realized that his boss or one of his co-workers would explicitly tell him if there was a memo that said something he needed to know. The employee found his workload reduced to slightly less than fifty hours per week. He was productive and happy.

One day, a memo came. It said at the top, "Important: Please Read." A little more than halfway through, on page twenty-seven, there was a description of a new law that had been passed, and how it required several jobs (including his own) to be done in a slightly different manner. Unfortunately, our friend's boss was in bed with a bad stomach flu, and so she wasn't able to tell him he needed to read the memo. So he continued doing his job as usual.

A year later, the company found itself the defendant in a forty million dollar lawsuit, and traced the negligence to the action of one single employee -- our friend. He was fired, and made the central villain in the storm of bad publicity.

But he definitely was in the wrong, and deserved what was coming to him. The administration very clearly explained the liability and his responsibility, in a memo very clearly labelled "Important". And he didn't even *read* the memo. It's his fault, right?

No.

Every communication that is sent to a person constitutes an implicit claim of, "This concerns you and is worth your attention." If experience tells other people that we lie again and again when we say this, then what right do we have to be believed when we really do have something important to say?

I retold the story of the boy who cried wolf as the story of the administrator who cried important, because administrators are among the worst offenders, along with lawyers, spammers, and perhaps people who pass along e-mail forwards. Among the stack of paper I was expected to sign when I moved in to my apartment was a statement that I had tested my smoke detector. The apartment staff was surprised that I wanted to test my smoke detector before signing my name to that statement. When an authority figure is surprised when a person reads a statement carefully and doesn't want to sign a claim that all involved know to be false, it's a bad sign.

There is communication that concerns the person it's directed to, but says too much -- for example, most of the legal contracts I've seen. The tiny print used to print many of those contracts constitutes an implicit acknowledment that the signer is not expected to read it: they don't even use the additional sheets of paper necessary to print text at a size that a person who only has 20/20 vision can easily read. There is also communication that is broadcast to many people who have no interest in it. To that communication, I would propose the following rule: *Do not, without exceptionally good reason, broadcast a communication that concerns only a minority of its recipients.* It's OK every now and then to announce that the blue Toyota with license place ABC 123 has its lights on. It's not OK to have a regular announcement that broadcasts anything that is approved as having interest to some of the recipients.

My church, which I am in general very happy with, has succumbed to vice by adding a section to the worship liturgy called "Announcements", where someone reads a list of events and such just before the end of the service, and completely dispels the moment that has been filling the sanctuary up until the announcements start. They don't do this with other things -- the offering is announced by music (usually good music) that contributes to the reverent atmosphere of the service. But when the service is drawing to a close, the worshipful atmosphere is disrupted by announcements which I at least almost never find useful. If the same list were printed on a sheet of paper, I could read it after the service, in less time, with greater comprehension, with zero disruption to the moment that every other part of the service tries so carefully to build -- and I could skip over any announcements that begin "For Married Couples:" or "Attention Junior High and High Schoolers!" The only advantage I can see to the present practice, from the church leadership's perspective, is that many people will not read the announcements at all if they have a choice about it -- and maybe, just *maybe*, there's a lesson in that.

As well as pointing out examples of a rampant problem in communication, where an administrator cries "Important!" over many things that are not worth reading, and then wonders why people don't believe him when he cries "Important!" about something which *is* important, I would like to suggest an alternative for communities that have access to the internet. A web server could use a form to let people select areas of concern and interest, and announcements submitted would be categorized, optionally cleared with a moderator, and sent only to those people who are interested in them. Another desirable feature might let end receivers select how much announcement information they can receive in a day -- providing a discernible incentive to the senders to minimize trivial communication. In a sense, this is what happens already -- intercom litanies of announcements ignored by school students in a classroom, employees carrying memos straight from their mailboxes to the recycle bins -- but in this case, administrators receive clear incentive and choice to conserve bandwidth and only send stuff that is genuinely important.

While I'm giving my Utopian dreams, I'd like to comment that at least some of this functionality is already supported by the infrastructure developed by UseNet. Probably there are refinements that can be implemented in a web interface -- all announcements for one topic shown from a single web page, since they shouldn't be nearly as long as a normal UseNet post arguing some obscure detail in an ongoing discussion. Perhaps other and better can be done -- I am suggesting "Here's something better than the status quo," not "Here's something so perfect that there's no room for improvement."

In one UseNet newsgroup, an exchange occurred that broadcasters of announcements would be well-advised to keep in mind. One person said, "I'm trying to decide whether to give the UseNet Bore of the Year Award to [name] or [name]. The winner will receive, as his prize, a copy of all of their postings, minutely inscribed, and rolled up inside a two foot poster tube."

Someone else posted a reply asking, "Length or diameter?"

To those of you who broadcast to people whom you are able to address because of your position and not because they have chosen to receive your broadcasts, I have the following to say: In each communication you send, you are deciding the basis by which people will decide if future communications are worth paying attention to, or just unwanted noise. If your noise deafens their ears, you have no right to complain that the few truly important things you have to tell them fall on deaf ears. **Only you can prevent spam!**

Christian Koans

A master observed that a novice was involved in many kinds of service and all kinds of good works. The master asked the novice, "Why do you do so many good works?"

"Because I am trying to make myself acceptable to God," the novice said.

The master set a tile before the novice, and began to polish it.

"What are you doing?", the novice asked.

"I am polishing this tile, to make it into a mirror."

"You can't make a tile into a mirror by polishing it!", the novice protested.

"And neither can you make yourself acceptable to God by good works," the master answered.

A scholar wrote an article saying, "The Bible shows evidence of post editing and was heavily influenced by the political climate of the day. Its interpretation depends highly on one's perspective."

A believer read the article, and said, "This article shows evidence of post editing and was heavily influenced by the political climate of the day. Its interpretation depends highly on one's perspective."

A man came to a believer and said, "You say that you know

God exists. Prove it to me."

The believer said, "Do you have any matches?"

"Yes."

The believer took a napkin, and soaked it in water. "You say that you have matches. Set this napkin on fire."

Someone said to a believer, "If God performed a miracle in front of me, I would believe."

The believer held up a blade of grass.

A novice closed his eyes, folded his hands, and began to say, "Our Father, who art in Heaven..."

A master said, "What are you doing?"

"I am assuming the right posture and saying the right words to pray."

"You can't pray by assuming a posture and saying a specific set of words."

"Then how do you pray?"

The master closed his eyes, folded his hands, and began, "Our Father, who art in Heaven..."

A master saw a novice gulping from a bottle of wine. "What are you doing?", the master said.

"I had a really rough day. I need a drink."

The master threw the wine against a wall. "Never drink wine because you need to."

"Do you drink wine?", the novice asked.

"Yes."

"Why?"

"Because I do not need to."

A Catholic and a Protestant were having a debate about faith and works, versus faith which works. Someone looked on, and said, "Everything is subject to debate. There is no core of universal Christian faith."

A believer punched him between the eyes.

"What did you do that for?", he asked.

"My fist looked different to your two eyes. Therefore, I did not hit you."

A novice said to a master, "I want to be a great man. What is the first thing I should do?"

The master answered, "Forget about being a great man."

A novice asked a master, "How am I to resist temptation? My strongest efforts of willpower are not enough."

The master asked the novice, "How am I to put out that fire? All the gasoline I own is not enough."

A novice said to a master, "Which do you value more: the truth, or the ancient Christian way?"

The master grabbed the novice's nose.

"Your response makes no sense," said the novice.

"And neither does your question," answered the master.

A novice said to a master, "I want to be totally devoted to God. Tell me how I should talk, how I should dress, how I should act."

The master said to the novice, "I want to be spontaneous. Tell me how I should plan my day."

A novice said to a master, "I am humble."

The master said, "No, you are not humble."

Another novice said, "I am not humble."

The master said, "That's right; you are not humble."

A novice handed a master a check, saying, "Here is some money, so that you will be happy."

The master put the check into the fire: "I wish the fire to be happy as well."

A computer professional said to a master, "I'm tired of wasting my time doing little things for God. I want to do something big and important."

The master said, "Tell me how to use a computer."

The professional said, "Well, first you turn it on, then y-"

The master interrupted him. "Don't waste my time talking about turning it on. I only want to know the important stuff."

A novice said to a master, "Where should I go to meet with God?"

The master said, "The radiator vent you are standing on."

A novice said to a master, "Tell me how to find deep, hidden secrets. I want to know beyond what is given to ordinary people to know."

The master said, "There are piles of diamonds out in the open. Why do you go lurking in caves, chasing after fool's gold?"

A novice said to a master, "I am sick and tired of the immorality that is all around us. There is fornication everywhere, drunkenness and drugs in the inner city, relativism in people's minds, and do you know where the worst of it is?"

The master said, "Inside your heart."

A man went to a cathedral where he had heard many miracles had occurred, visions of Heaven. "I have come all the way from America, to find God," he told one of the believers.

"Aah. God has gone all the way to America, to find you."

A novice once said to a master who was maimed, "Do you ever ask, 'Why me?'"

The master said, "Yes, frequently. I ask God every day why he has given me so many blessings."

A master was working at a soup kitchen, serving food, talking with the guests, listening to their stories.

"What are you doing?", a novice asked.

"I am praying and telling God how much I love him."

Later, after everyone had left, the master folded his hands, and said, "God, you are so awesome. Thank you for making me your child. I love you. Thank you for..."

The novice asked, "What are you doing?"

The master said, "I am loving God's precious children."

Someone said to a master, "What about the people who have never heard of Christ? Are they all automatically damned to Hell? Tell me; I have heard that you have studied this question."

The master said, "What you need to be saved is for you to believe in Christ, and you have heard of him."

A feminist theologian said to a master, "I think it is important that we keep an open mind and avoid confining God to traditional categories of gender."

The master said, "Of course. Why let God reveal himself as masculine when you can confine him to your canons of political correctness?"

A novice said to a master, "My master, teach me!"

The master said, "How can I teach you? I am a novice, and you are a master."

A novice and a master were walking together. The master said, "Oh, how it distresses God to see all the heresies and schisms in the Church."

The novice said, "How do you know what God feels? You're not God."

The master said, "How do you know whether or not I know what God feels? You're not me."

A novice said to a master, "I wish that Christ were still around, that we could love him."

The master picked up a little girl, and gave her a kiss.

One person said, "The Christian message is narrow-minded of different belief systems."

Another said, "No, it is Christian missionaries and evangelists who are narrow-minded and intolerant of any different belief system."

A master said, "Neither of you are right. It is you who are narrow-minded and intolerant of any really different belief system."

A novice said to a master, "I want to serve God. What denomination should I join?"

The master said, "I want to be healthy. What part of my body should I cut off?"

Someone said to a master, "God is love, so he can't condemn homosexual practice."

The master said, "Doctors want people to be healthy, so they can't call cancer 'sickness'."

A novice said to a master, "Take me to your highest priest."

The master introduced him to each believer present, saying, "This is the highest priest. You will not find a more sacred priest."

A novice asked a master, "Do you believe that some days are especially holy, or that all days are equally holy?"

The master said, "Yes."

A novice asked a master, "How should I empty my mind of lust?"

The master said, "Fill it with Christ."

A physicist said to a master, "I believe my own private religion, which I design to suit me, provide me with meaning, and make me happy. What better suited religion can you possibly claim to have?"

The master began to write on a sheet of paper, "Gravity shall pull things together except on Tuesdays and Thursdays, when gravity shall have no effects whatsoever. Objects at rest tend to begin to move; objects in motion tend to ..."

"What on earth are you writing?", the novice said,

"I believe my own private physics, which I design to suit me, provide me with meaning, and make me happy. What better suited physics can you possibly claim to have?"

A wealthy novice came to a master, and said, "Teach me!"

The master said, "Scrub out all the wastebaskets."

The novice scrubbed out the wastebaskets and returned. The master did not give a word of thanks, so much as a smile. "Now weed the garden."

The novice weeded the garden and returned. The master did not give a word of thanks, so much as a smile. "Now give us your car."

The novice gave him his car, and then said in frustration, "Why haven't you shown so much as a hint of gratitude? I have done menial service and given you my own car. Isn't that a lot?"

The master said, "Yes, it is a lot, but we need neither your service nor your car. You came to us proud and accustomed to luxury. We gave you an opportunity to taste humble service. We gave you an opportunity to let go of a cherished possession. It is you who should be grateful."

Someone said to a master, "Come to our forum. We talk and debate, and express our values and opinions. There is complete freedom, and anybody can believe anything he likes."

The master said, "Do you masturbate?"

A shocked voice said, "What?"

The master calmly clarified, "Do you do with your genitals what you boast of doing with your mind?"

Someone said to a master, "I want to believe in God. Persuade me, so that I can believe."

The master said, "I want you to be filled, but I can never eat enough to satisfy your hunger."

A philosopher said to a master, "Our judgements can err. I try to doubt things and disbelieve what cannot be proven, so that I will not hold false beliefs."

The master closed his eyes.

"What are you doing?", the philosopher asked.

"When I walk, I sometimes bump into things," the master explained. "I am closing my eyes so that the room will be empty."

A novice came to a master, talking about the many evil things that stained Church history. After he had finished, the master said, "May I pour you a Coke?"

"Sure."

The master returned with a glass full of icewater, and a two liter bottle of soda. He opened the bottle, poured until the glass was full to the brim - and then kept on pouring. The liquid flowed over the edges of the glass, pouring all over the gable, and spilled onto the floor.

"Stop!", the novice protested. "What are you doing?"

"This glass cannot have any more soda poured into it until it is first emptied. And neither can you grasp the truth until you let go of thinking of the Church as you do now."

A CEO sent a business card to a master, listing his name and title. The master sent a novice, saying, "Send him away. I have no time to waste with such a person!"

The visitor then scratched out his title and degrees, sending the card back with only his name.

"Aah, send him in!", the master said. "I have been longing to meet that fellow."

A visiting liberal theologian was talking with a master and said, "We have found a way of interpreting the whole Bible that is in accordance with our progressive and liberated beliefs."

At that moment, the power went out, and the room was plunged into darkness.

"Just a minute," the master said, and returned with a candle and some matches. He lit the candle, and they talked for a while longer.

After a time, the theologian wanted to get off to bed, and the master said, "Here, take this candle; it will light your way so that you will not stumble."

As the visitor received the candle, the master blew it out.

A visiting novice said to a master, "I have been taught to carefully live by rules and not do anything that might cause me trouble, in order that I not do wrong."

The master took a heavy stone, and dropped it on a small crystalline statuette, crushing it to dust. "I have protected that statue with a great stone, so that nothing can harm it."

A novice asked a master, "Have you made much progress over what the Church used to believe in ancient times?"

The master said, "None of us considers himself wise enough to do better than what God has declared to be true. Do you?"

A novice asked a master, "Are you Catholic or Protestant?"

The master said, "Yes. No. Both."

The novice said, "Please. It will help me better understand where you are coming from."

The master said, "Is the elephant in your closet eating peanut butter? Answer me now, yes or no."

"If I say either 'yes' or 'no'," the novice protested, "I will deceive you and set back your understanding greatly."

"And if I say either 'Catholic' or 'Protestant'," the master answered, "I also will deceive you and set your understanding back greatly. I am a Christian. If you think anything more, you will know less."

A novice told a master, "I am going to seminary."

"Why?", the master asked.

"To become well-versed in Scripture and Christian doctrine."

The master began to walk out of the room.

"Where are you going?", the novice asked.

"I am going to the garage," the master answered.

"Why?", the novice asked.

"To become a car."

Someone challenged a master, saying, "The Bible and Christian tradition say, first, that God the Creator is all powerful, second, that God the Creator is all good, third, that God the

Creator is all wise, and fourth, that there is evil in God's creation now.

"These contradict each other, so one of them must be false. Which one do you deny?"

The master said, "I deny the one that says that your mind has the power, the wisdom, and the authority to put God in a box and say, 'These contradict each other, so one of them must be false. You're wrong, God.'"

"And in conclusion," the speaker said, "truly understanding the overall teaching of Scripture requires that one disregard problematic passages such as the 'Do not resist evil.' in the Sermon on the Mount that was brought up earlier."

"I agree completely," the master said, "To get a good view of the forest, it is essential to chop down all the trees that keep obstructing your view."

Someone told a master, "I memorize the Scriptures so that I will be able to answer anyone who comes to me, with the very words of God."

The master said, "Let me tell you about that painting on the wall," and described in perfect detail every hue, every brush stroke.

"Very well," the visitor said, "but what is the painting a picture of?"

"Very well," the master said, "but what is the Bible about?"

A novice asked a master, "Can't God let even one of the damned enter into Heaven?"

The master said, "By the time the damned will enter Hell, they will be so steeped in evil that even Heaven would be Hell to them."

A novice said to a master, "How can I reach up to God?"

The master said, "Let God reach down to you."

A Star Trek fan told a master, "Christianity is like the Borg, sucking in every nation and race it can, making them like itself. I, for one, refuse to be assimilated."

The master hung his head. "It is so sad."

"What is so sad? That Christianity wants to assimilate me? That I refuse to be assimilated?"

"That the Borg has already assimilated you, and you believe it to be perfection."

Religion Within the Bounds of Amusement

On the screen appear numerous geometrical forms--prisms, cylinders, cubes -- dancing, spinning, changing shape, in a very stunning computer animation. In the background sounds the pulsing beat of techno music. The forms waver, and then coalesce into letters: "Religion Within the Bounds of Amusement."

The music and image fade, to reveal a man, perfect in form and appearance, every hair in place, wearing a jet black suit and a dark, sparkling tie. He leans forward slightly, as the camera focuses in on him.

"Good morning, and I would like to extend a warm and personal welcome to each and every one of you from those of us at the Church of the Holy Television. Please sit back, relax, and turn off your brain."

Music begins to play, and the screen shows a woman holding a microphone. She is wearing a long dress of the whitest white, the color traditionally symbolic of goodness and purity, which somehow manages not to conceal her unnaturally large breasts. The camera slowly focuses in as she begins to sing.

"You got problems? That's OK. You got problems? That's OK. Not enough luxury? That's OK. Only three cars? That's OK. Not enough power? That's OK. Can't get your way? That's OK. Not enough for you? That's OK. Can't do it on your own? That's

OK. You got problems? That's OK. You got problems? That's OK. Just call out to Jesus, and he'll make them go away. Just call out to Jesus, and he'll make them go away."

As the music fades, the camera returns to the man.

"Have you ever thought about how much God loves us? Think about the apex of progress that we are at, and how much more he has blessed us than any one else.

"The Early Christians were in a dreadful situation. They were always under persecution. Because of this, they didn't have the physical assurance of security that is the basis for spiritual growth, nor the money to buy the great libraries of books that are necessary to cultivate wisdom. It is a miracle that Christianity survived at all.

"The persecution ended, but darkness persisted for a thousand years. The medievals were satisfied with blind faith, making it the context of thought and leisure. Their concept of identity was so weak that it was entangled with obedience. The time was quite rightly called the Dark Ages.

"But then, ah, the Renaissance and the Enlightenment. Man and his mind enthroned. Religion within the bounds of reason. Then science and technology, the heart of all true progress, grew.

"And now, we sit at the apex, blessed with more and better technology than anyone else. What more could you possibly ask for? What greater blessing could there possibly be? We have the technology, and know how to enjoy it. Isn't God gracious?"

There is a dramatic pause, and then the man closes his eyes. "Father, I thank you that we have not fallen into sin; that we do not worship idols, that we do not believe lies, and that we are not like the Pharisees. I thank you that we are good, moral people; that we are Americans. I thank you, and I praise you for your wondrous power. Amen."

He opens his eyes, and turns to the camera. It focuses in on his face, and his piercing gaze flashes out like lightning. With a thunderous voice, he boldly proclaims, "To God alone be the glory, for ever and ever!"

The image fades.

In the background can be heard the soft tones of Beethoven. A couple fades in; they are elegantly dressed, sitting at a black marble table, set with roast pheasant. The room is of Baroque fashion; marble pillars and mirrors with gilt frames adorn the walls. French windows overlook a formal garden.

The scene changes, and a sleek black sports car glides through forest, pasture, village, mountain. The music continues to play softly.

It passes into a field, and in the corner of the field a small hovel stands. The camera comes closer, and two half-naked children come into view, playing with some sticks and a broken Coca-Cola bottle. Their heads turn and follow the passing car.

A voice gently intones, "These few seconds may be the only opportunity some people ever have to know about you. What do you want them to see?"

The picture changes. Two men are walking through a field. As the camera comes closer, it is seen that they are deep in conversation.

One of them looks out at the camera with a probing gaze, and then turns to the other. "What do you mean?"

"I don't know, Jim." He draws a deep breath, and closes his eyes. "I just feel so... so empty. A life filled with nothing but shallowness. Like there's nothing inside, no purpose, no meaning. Just an everlasting nothing."

"Well, you know, John, for every real and serious problem, there is a solution which is trivial, cheap, and instantaneous." He unslings a small backpack, opening it to pull out two cans of beer, and hands one to his friend. "Shall we?"

The cans are opened.

Suddenly, the peaceful silence is destroyed by the blare of loud rock music. The camera turns upwards to the sky, against which may be seen parachutists; it spins, and there is suddenly a large swimming pool, and a vast table replete with great pitchers and kegs of beer. The parachutists land; they are all young women, all blonde, all laughing and smiling, all wearing string bikinis, and all anorexic.

For the remaining half of the commercial, the roving camera takes a lascivious tour of the bodies of the models. Finally, the image fades, and a deep voice intones, "Can you think of a better way to spend your weekends?"

The picture changes. A luxury sedan, passing through a ghetto, stops beside a black man, clad in rags. The driver, who is white, steps out in a pristine business suit, opens his wallet, and pulls out five crisp twenty dollar bills.

"I know that you can't be happy, stealing, lying, and getting drunk all of the time. Here is a little gift to let you know that Jesus loves you." He steps back into the car without waiting to hear the man's response, and speeds off.

Soon, he is at a house. He steps out of the car, bible in hand, and rings the doorbell.

The door opens, and a man says, "Nick, how are you? Come in, do come in. Have a seat. I was just thinking of you, and it is so nice of you to visit. May I interest you in a little Martini?"

Nick sits down and says, "No, Scott. I am a Christian, and we who are Christian do not do such things."

"Aah; I see." There is a sparkle in the friend's eye as he continues, "And tell me, what did Jesus do at his first miracle?"

The thick, black, leatherbound 1611 King James bible arcs through the air, coming to rest on the back of Scott's head. There is a resounding thud.

"You must learn that the life and story of Jesus are serious matters, and not to be taken as the subject of jokes."

The screen turns white as the voice glosses, "This message has been brought to you by the Association of Concerned Christians, who would like to remind you that you, too, can be different from the world, and can present a positive witness to Christ."

In the studio again, the man is sitting in a chair.

"Now comes a very special time in our program. You, our viewers, matter most to us. It is your support that keeps us on the air. And I hope that you do remember to send us money; when you do, God will bless you. So keep your checks rolling, and we will be able to continue this ministry, and provide answers to your questions. I am delighted to be able to hear your phone calls. Caller number one, are you there?"

"Yes, I am, and I would like to say how great you are. I sent you fifty dollars, and someone gave me an anonymous check for five hundred! I only wish I had given you more."

"That is good to hear. God is so generous. And what is your question?"

"I was wondering what God's will is for America? And what I can do to help?"

"Thank you; that's a good question.

"America is at a time of great threat now; it is crumbling because good people are not elected to office.

"The problem would be solved if Christians would all listen to Rush Limbaugh, and then go out and vote. Remember, bad people are sent to Washington by good people who don't vote. With the right men in office, the government would stop wasting its time on things like the environment, and America would become a great and shining light, to show all the world what Christ can do.

"Caller number two?"

"I have been looking for a church to go to, and having trouble. I just moved, and used to go to a church which had nonstop stories and anecdotes; the congregation was glued to the edges of their seats. Here, most of the services are either boring or have something which lasts way too long. I have found a few churches whose services I generally enjoy--the people really sing the songs--but there are just too many things that aren't amusing. For starters, the sermons make me uncomfortable, and for another, they have a very boring time of silent meditation, and this weird mysticism about 'kiss of peace' and something to do with bread and wine. Do you have any advice for me?"

"Yes, I do. First of all, what really matters is that you have Jesus in your heart. Then you and God can conquer the world. Church is a peripheral; it doesn't really have anything to do with Jesus being in your heart. If you find a church that you like, go for it, but if there aren't any that you like, it's not your fault that they aren't doing their job.

"And the next caller?"

"Hello. I was wondering what the Song of Songs is about."

"The Song of Songs is an allegory of Christ's love for the Church. Various other interpretations have been suggested, but they are all far beyond the bounds of good taste, and read things into the text which would be entirely inappropriate in holy Scriptures. Next caller?"

"My people has a story. I know tales of years past, of soldiers come, of pillaging, of women ravaged, of villages razed to the ground and every living soul murdered by men who did not hesitate to wade through blood. Can you tell me what kind of religion could possibly decide that the Crusades were holy?"

The host, whose face had suddenly turned a deep shade of red, shifted slightly, and pulled at the side of his collar. After a few seconds, a somewhat less polished voice hastily states, "That would be a very good question to answer, and I really would like to, but I have lost track of time. It is now time for an important message from some of our sponsors."

The screen is suddenly filled by six dancing rabbits, singing about toilet paper.

A few minutes of commercials pass: a computer animated flash of color, speaking of the latest kind of candy; a family brought together and made happy by buying the right brand of vacuum cleaner; a specific kind of hamburger helping black and white, young and old to live together in harmony. Somewhere in there, the Energizer bunny appears; one of the people in the scene tells the rabbit that he should have appeared at some time other than the commercial breaks. Finally, the host, who has regained his composure, is on the screen again.

"Well, that's all for this week. I hope you can join us next week, as we begin a four part series on people whose lives have been changed by the Church of the Holy Television. May God bless you, and may all of your life be ever filled with endless amusement!"

So You've Hired a Hacker (Revised and Expanded)

There is a wonderful variety among humans. Ethnicity and culture provide one of the most important dimensions--but there can be profound differences between two people who look the same. If neither appreciates the differences, and thinks, "He's just like me--only not doing a very good job of it," there will be conflicts that can be prevented. If they understand their differences, both can profit. This document is written so that you can understand your hacker and enjoy a more productive working relationship.

Managers and hackers both vary, but there are some things that come up again and again. That's why this document exists. I am concerned with a particular kind of clash that most hackers have with many managers--a conflict that is more easily resolved if both parties understand each other.

What are some of the common differences between managers and hackers? There are several, but let me list five important ones:

Managers	Hackers

Tends to be very concerned with morality, and wants to connect with society and contribute. Rises to positions of responsibility, not only in business, but in church and volunteer organizations. Lives by responsibility and duty.	Intent on cultivating knowledge and skill. Rises to tremendous levels of competency with technology and other things. High level of discipline used to continually refine abilities.
Thinks concretely. Good at small talk, and at the logistical details needed to run a business.	Thinks abstractly. Good at deep discussions, and thinking about the hard concepts needed to work with technology.
Measures own contribution to society by the extent to which he adds to rules and sees that people live by following rules. Tends to equate rules with morality or the	Far more aware of the limitations of rules. Does not equate rules with morality or the good of society. Very likely to notice rules that are hurting your company--yes, they

good of society.	*do* exist, and they're more common than you think.
Closely resembles about 40% of the population; most people have dealt with many similar people before, and can easily understand managers.	Thinks in an uncommon way found in perhaps 5% of the population; will encounter many people who have never known well anyone who is similar. Can't count on other people understanding him.
Is such a dominant force in human society that he can easily forget that others might be different. Works well with people because of how much he holds in common with so many others. Needs to work at understanding people like hackers.	May have intense powers of concentration. Prizes an offbeat and clever sense of humor. At times, painfully aware of inconsistencies that are invisible to the people who are acting hypocritically. Marches to the beat of a different drummer, and needs to work at understanding

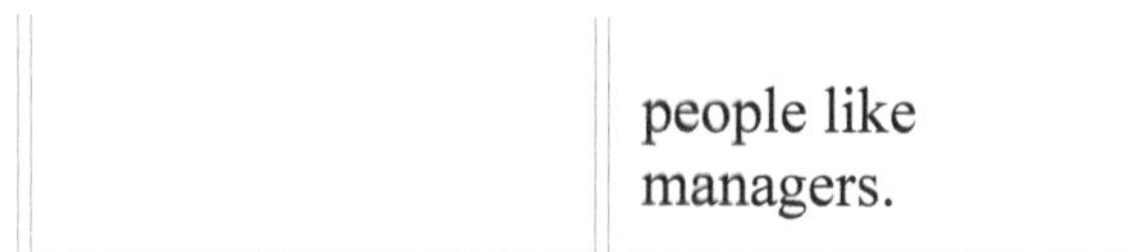

	people like managers.

Managers and hackers complement each other. If they work at it, they can enjoy a long and fruitful working relationship.

Questions and Answers:

Section 1: Basic Understanding

1.1: Won't my hacker break into my computer and steal my trade secrets?

Point of clarification. There are *two* communities of people that call themselves 'hackers'.

One of these groups is the one you've heard about--those who take pride in breaking into other people's computers. That is all the media understands 'hacker' to mean, but there is another community, an older and much more interesting one, that is insulted by being mistaken for the first community. They are as insulted as an automotive engineer would be if the media said 'automotive engineer' when they meant 'car thief', and the engineer learned through bitter experience that, whenever he told people he was an automotive engineer, people thought he was only a car thief.

Your hacker is an automotive engineer, not a car thief. He is a hacker because he loves computers, and loves to do impressive things with them. He doesn't want to steal your trade secrets, and it would be good manners of you not to confuse "automotive engineer" hackers with "car thief" hackers--whom he refers to as 'crackers', or the extremely pejorative 'script kiddies'.

1.2: Was it a good idea to hire a hacker?

It depends on the job. A hacker can be dramatically more

effective than a non-hacker at a job, or dramatically less effective. Jobs where hackers are particularly good are:

- Systems administration
- Programming
- Design
- Web-related development

Jobs where hackers are particularly bad are:

- Data entry
- "Computer operator", where the "computer operator" has to use software (especially MicroSoft software) that he can't improve.

More generally, a job that requires fast and unexpected changes, significant skill, talent, and is not very repetitive will be one a hacker will excel at. Repetitive, simple jobs are a waste of a good hacker, and will make your hacker bored and frustrated. No one works well bored and frustrated.

The good news is, if you get a hacker on something he particularly likes, you will frequently see performance on the order of five to ten times what a "normal" worker would produce. This is not consistent, and you shouldn't expect to see it all the time, but it will happen. This is most visible on particularly difficult tasks.

1.3 Wait, you just said "ten times", didn't you? You're not serious, right?

Yes, I am serious; a hacker on a roll may be able to produce, in a period of a few months, something that a small development group (say, 7-8 people) would have a hard time getting together over a year. He also may not. Your mileage will vary.

IBM used to report that certain programmers might be as much as 100 times as productive as other workers, or more. This kind of thing happens.

1.4 How should I manage my hacker?

The same way you herd cats. It can be quite confusing; they're not like most other workers. Don't worry! Your hacker is likely to be willing to suggest answers to problems, if asked. Hackers are known for coming together and producing impressive software without any business people to tell them what to do. That's how Perl was produced. And Linux. And quite a few other things, great and small. Most hackers are nearly self-managing.

1.5 I don't understand this at all. This is confusing. Is there a book on this?

There are several books that explain important pieces of the puzzle, and some of them are listed in a reading list below. If you read from the list and ask your hacker to help you connect the dots, you've got a good chance at understanding your hacker much better.

Section 2: Social issues

2.1: My hacker doesn't fit in well with our corporate society. She seems to do her work well, but she's not really making many friends.

This is common. Your hacker may not have found any people around who get along with hackers. You may wish to consider offering her a position telecommuting, or flexible hours (read: night shift), which may actually improve her productivity. Or, even better, hire another one.

2.2: My hacker seems to dress funny. Is there any way to impress upon him the importance of corporate appearance?

Well... let's look at your view of clothing first, so that you'll have a better chance at understanding how your hacker sees things differently.

You believe in showing respect for the company and those you work with. To you, much of that respect revolves around little details. These details are to you much of the substance of respect--such as that classy suit you wear to the office. So when a hacker wears jeans and a t-shirt to work, he must be showing disrespect, right?

Not really. Those jeans--kneeholes and all--are what he wears to see his best friend, whom he respects deeply. If your hacker happens to be a Christian, he may wear jeans and a T-shirt to church on Easter. I sometimes do, and when I dress up for church, it is more to avoid distracting other churchgoers than any need of fancy clothes in order to worship God. Hackers look past appearances, and it seems strange to them that you think they need uncomfortable clothes to work well: if it's what's inside the clothing that matters, why not wear something comfortable and be able to concentrate better?

If your hacker isn't dressing up, how can he still respect your company? He works hard, solves problems, and probably thinks about ways to help your company be more productive--even when he's at home. If he wants to wear comfortable clothing at work, it's not disrespect; he just understands what IBM, MicroSoft, and Ford all recognize: employees are most productive when they choose what to wear--not their company. If you ask your hacker respectfully, he'll probably wear clothing without any holes, and might even dress up for a few special occasions.

Your suit is a professional asset. It helps other people see your professionalism. Your hacker's t-shirt is also a professional asset. It's part of a culture that judges a person by what's *inside* his clothing, and he works better when comfortable. He doesn't try to get you to dress like him; why don't you extend the same courtesy to him?

2.3: My hacker won't call me by my title, and doesn't seem to respect me at all.

Your hacker doesn't respect your title. Hackers don't believe that management is "above" engineering; they believe that management is doing one job, and engineering is doing another. They may well frequently talk as if management is beneath them, but this is really quite fair; your question implies that you talk as if engineering is beneath you. Treat your hacker as an equal, and she will probably treat you as an equal!

2.4: My hacker constantly insults the work of my other workers.

Take your hacker aside, and ask for details of what's wrong with the existing work. It may be that there's something wrong with it. Don't let the fact that it runs most of the time fool you; your hacker is probably bothered by the fact that it crashes at all. As your customers will be--consider your hacker to be an early warning system. He may be able to suggest improvements which could dramatically improve performance, reliability, or other features. It's worth looking into.

You may be able to convince your hacker to be more polite, but if there appear to be major differences, it's quite possible that one or more of your existing staff are incompetent by his standards. Note that hackers, of course, have different standards of competence than many other people. (Read "different" as "much higher".) Is this necessarily appropriate? All people have weaknesses. It would perhaps be nicer if hackers were more charitable to people who can't match their talent, but you're lucky to have someone on staff who's competent enough for this to be a problem.

Section 3: Productivity

3.1: My hacker plays video games on company time.

Abraham Lincoln said, "If I had ten hours to chop down an oak tree, I'd spend the first eight sharpening my axe."

Some jobs are done best by getting your hands dirty immediately: if you hire a kid to rake your leaves, you probably want him to start raking as soon as he arrives. But if you contacted a building contractor to make a new office building in the morning, and he was pouring concrete by the end of the day, you would not be impressed--at least not in a good way. Something is very wrong: there are all sorts of things that need to happen first. If your contractor begins work by pouring concrete, you will end up paying for some very expensive mistakes that could have been completely avoided by simple preparation.

Your hacker is probably honest, too honest to start off by writing poor-quality code "so my manager will think I'm working." He'd rather be productive and spend two weeks preparing rather than two years fixing needless mistakes.

Perhaps it would be easier if hacker ways of preparation coincided with what you do when working--writing memos or something like that. But there is an elusive productive zone, and your hacker is doing whatever he can to gain that productivity. I often write best after taking meandering walks. Your hacker who plays games on company time is using the same areas of his mind as I did. Your hacker is sharpening his axe, and it's a good idea for him to do so.

Hackers, writers, and painters all need some amount of time to spend "percolating"--doing something else to let their subconscious work on a problem. Your hacker is probably stuck on something difficult. Don't worry about it.

3.2: But it's been two weeks since I saw anything!

Your hacker is working, alone probably, on a big project, and just started, right? She's probably trying to figure it all out in advance. Ask her how it's going; if she starts a lot of sentences, but interrupts them all with "no, wait..." or "drat, that won't work", it's going well.

3.3: Isn't this damaging to productivity?

No. Your hacker needs to recreate and think about things in many ways. He will be more productive with this recreation than without it. Your hacker enjoys working; don't worry about things getting done reasonably well and quickly.

3.4: My hacker is constantly doing things unrelated to her job responsibilities.

Do they need to be done? Very few hackers can resist solving a problem when they can solve it, and no one else is solving it. For that matter, is your hacker getting her job done? If so, consider these other things a freebie or perk (for you). Although it may not be conventional, it's probably helping out quite a bit.

3.5: My hacker is writing a book, reading USENET news, playing video games, talking with friends on the phone, and building sculptures out of paper clips. On company time!

He sounds happy. The chances are he's in one of three states:

- Basic job responsibilities are periodic (phone support, documentation, et al.) and there's a lull in incoming work. Don't worry about it!
- Your hacker is stuck on a difficult problem.
- Your hacker is bored silly and is trying to find amusement. Perhaps you should find him more challenging work?

Any of these factors may be involved. All of them may be involved. In general, if the work is challenging, and is getting done, don't worry too much about the process. You might ask for your corporation to be given credit in the book.

3.6: But my other workers are offended by my hacker's success, and it hurts their productivity.

Do you really need to have workers around who would rather be the person getting something done, than have it done already? Ego has very little place in the workplace. If they can't do it well, assign them to something they can do.

Section 4: Stimulus and response

4.1: My hacker did something good, and I want to reward him.

Good! Here are some of the things most hackers would like to receive in exchange for their work:

- Understanding.
- Understanding.
- Understanding.
- Respect.
- Admiration.
- Compliments.
- Discounts on expensive toys.
- Money.

The order is approximate, but the most important one is the most difficult. If you can give that to your hacker, in his eyes you will be a cut above most other bosses--and he just might work for you longer.

Try to remember this good thing your hacker just did the next time you discover he just spent a day playing x-trek. Rather than complaining about getting work done, write it off as "a perk" that was granted (informally) as a bonus for a job well done. Don't worry; hackers get bored quickly when they aren't doing their work.

4.2: My hacker did something bad, and I want to punish him.

Don't. 30 years of psychological research has shown that punishment has no desirable long-term effects. Your hacker is not a lab rat. (Even if he *were* a lab rat, punishment wouldn't work; at least, not if he were one of the sorts of lab rats the psych research was done on.) If you don't like something your hacker is doing, express your concerns. Explain what it is that bothers you about the behavior.

Be prepared for an argument; your hacker is a rational entity, and presumably had reasons. Don't jump on him too quickly; they may turn out to be good reasons.

Don't be afraid to apologize if you're wrong. Your hacker will never think less of you if you admit to a mistake. He might be disappointed if you've made a mistake and can't admit it, but he will *never* look down on you for admitting you were wrong. If your hacker admits to being wrong, don't demand an additional apology; so far as the hacker is concerned, admitting to being wrong probably *is* an apology.

4.3: I don't get it. I offered my hacker a significant promotion, and she turned it down and acted offended.

A promotion frequently involves spending more time listening to people describing what they're doing, and less time playing with computers. Your hacker is enjoying her work; if you want to offer a reward, consider an improvement in title, a possible raise, and some compliments. Make sure your hacker knows you are pleased with her *accomplishments*--that's what she's there for.

4.4: My company policy won't let me give my hacker any more raises until he's in management.

In the Bible, Paul describes roles in the Christian church,

and then compares these community members to parts of the human body (I Corinthians 12:14-26, NIV):

Now the body is not made up of one part but of many. If the foot should say, "Because I am not a hand, I do not belong to the body," it would not for that reason cease to be part of the body. And if the ear should say, "Because I am not an eye, I do not belong to the body," it would not for that reason cease to be part of the body. If the whole body were an eye, where would the sense of hearing be? If the whole body were an ear, where would the sense of smell be? But in fact God has arranged the parts in the body, every one of them, just as he wanted them to be. If they were all one part, where would the body be? As it is, there are many parts, but one body.

The eye cannot say to the hand, "I don't need you!" And the head cannot say to the feet, "I don't need you!" On the contrary, those parts of the body that seem to be weaker are indispensable, and the parts that we think are less honorable we treat with special honor. And the parts that are unpresentable are treated with special modesty, while our presentable parts need no special treatment. But God has combined the members of the body and has given greater honor to the parts that lacked it, so that there should be no division in the body, but that its parts should have equal concern for each other. If one part suffers, every part suffers with it; if one part is honored, every part rejoices with it.

This is a deep insight into human community. It's not just about religion. Executives, managers, programmers, salespeople, secretaries, and other employees all contribute something fundamental to a company. *Janitors? Those* people are important? Well, if janitors aren't important, *fire* them, and streamline your business. The halls may be a bit stinky with all that rotting trash, and two of the secretaries may sneeze every time someone walks by and kicks up dust. Your insurance covers emergency treatment and rabies shots when a rat creeps out of a mound of garbage and bites you, right? Your star saleswoman couldn't close a key sale because she was in the hospital with food poisoning after... wait a minute. Maybe those janitors we all look down on deserve a second look. Maybe they contribute more to the physical well-being of other employees than almost anyone else you have on staff. Maybe they're important after all.

Eye, hand, stomach, and sturdy back muscles all contribute something. Sometimes the observation--"My group adds something unique and vital, something that no other department gives."--to a conclusion that is not justified: "My group's contribution to the company is better and more important than anyone else."

This conclusion also affects how companies allocate money: the people who set salaries believe they're the most important employees. Because it's management who sets the salaries, the belief:

> A manager is a more important employee than a non-manager

creates a policy like

> Every manager must be paid more than any non-manager

or

> No matter how much an employee does for the company, there's an artificial limit on how much you can reward him unless he gives up his work, which he is good at, and becomes a manager instead.

If that's what you believe--a prejudice that would *shock* any true leader--then I don't think I can help you much. I would simply encourage you to finish the job. Send a memo out to all employees saying:

> We believe that every manager makes a more important contribution to this company than any non-

manager. If you're not a manager, you're only a second-class citizen with our company. If you don't like this, you can leave.

And be ready for an exodus. Your hackers won't be the only ones to decide you're too stupid to work with. They'll just be the first.

Does that sound unattractive? You do have a better alternative. Your hacker can quite possibly earn $200/hour or more, if he wants--his talents are worth it. If your company policy imposes a salary ceiling on non-managers, *your company policy is broken*. Fix your company policy, find a loophole (say, a consultant given a contracted permament consulting position with benefits), or else get ready to have one of your most productive employees leave because your company policy is broken and you couldn't work around it.

I can't believe the hacker on my staff is worth as much as we're paying.

Ask the other in the staff what the hacker does, and what they think of it. The chances are that your hacker is spending a few hours a week answering arcane questions that would otherwise require an expensive external consultant. Your hacker may be fulfilling another job's worth of responsibilities in his spare time around the office. Very few hackers aren't worth what they're getting paid; they enjoy accomplishing difficult tasks, and improving worker efficiency.

Section 5: What does *that* mean?

5.1: My hacker doesn't speak English. At least, I don't *think* so.

Your hacker is a techie, and knows a number of powerful concepts that most English-speakers don't know. He also knows words for those concepts. Guess what? The concepts are unusual concepts, and the words are unusual words. He doesn't use standard words for many things because there aren't any standard words to explain the cool things he does.

Your best bet is to pick up a copy of TNHD (*The New Hacker's Dictionary*). It can be found at http://catb.org/jargon or from a good bookstore. If you have trouble understanding that reference, ask your hacker if she has a copy, or would be willing to explain her terms. Most hackers are willing to explain terms. Be ready for condescension; it's not intended as an insult, but if you don't know the words, she probably *has* to talk down to you at first to explain them. If you're bothered by this, think about explaining to a non-professional how to keep a project on task--*if you can't use any words longer than five letters*. That's what your hacker is doing when she tries to explain technical concepts in non-technical words. Please understand if she sounds a little condescending.

It's a reasonably difficult set of words; there are a lot of them, and their usage is much more precise than it sounds. Hackers love word games.

It is also possible that English is not your hacker's native language, and that it's not yours either. Feel free to substitute a more appropriate language.

5.2: I can't get an estimate out of my hacker.

This is easier to understand with an analogy. Imagine two situations:

In the first situation, you drive for work on the same roads, at the same time, as you have for the past five years, and listened to the traffic report in the shower.

In the second situation, you are out in the middle of nowhere, traveling to see a distant relative, and you realize that you've forgotten to buy a hostess gift for the people you're driving to visit. You stop by a gas station to ask where you can find a gift shop which would sell a dolphin statuette. The attendant says, "Take the road you're on, and turn off onto the second side street you see. Keep on going until you hit the second stop sign after John's general store. It's in the third town you'll see."

Now, in both cases, think about answering the question, "How long will it take?"

In the first case, you probably know the answer: "Twenty-six minutes, twenty-two if I hit the lights right." In the second case--well, given that you don't know how long the route is, what the speed limits are, or how you will find the sign once you reach the right town, the best answer is, "I don't know."

When you ask a hacker how long a task will take and he says, "I don't know," he isn't being difficult. Fixing a broken network, when you don't know why it's down, is much more like the second situation than the first. You don't need to throw a pity party for your hacker because he has to work in unfamiliar territory and doesn't even know how long a task will take. He doesn't look at it that way; he likes the challenge. But it does mean that he accepts tasks before he knows exactly how he'll do them, and he is responsible enough to say "I don't know," and not tell you something he's simply made up. Your hacker is a driver who thrives on finding his way in unfamiliar territory, with washed-out bridges and incomplete directions among the surprises. You might be glad you have someone who likes that kind of assignment.

Your hacker hasn't figured out how hard the problem is yet. Unlike most workers, hackers will try very hard to refuse to give an estimate until they know for sure that they understand the problem. This may include solving it.

No good engineer goes beyond 95% certainty. Most hackers are good engineers. If you say that you will not try to hold him to the estimate (and mean it!) you are much more likely to get an approximate estimate. The estimate may sound very high or very low; it may be very high or very low. Still, it's an estimate, and you get what you ask for.

5.3: My hacker makes obscure, meaningless jokes.

Another one that's a little hard to explain.

Imagine that you are visited by a brilliant wayfarer. He

strives to understand those around, silently tolerates a great many things that seem strange to him, and brings with him cultural treasures unlike anything your culture has to offer. One day, he tries to share some of them with you. Should you be bothered?

That's what's happening when your hacker tells you obscure technical jokes. He could be trying to make you feel stupid, but let's be charitable. Your hacker is uncommonly intelligent--he might be a member of Mensa. Intelligent people think a little bit differently, and a genius may seem like someone from another world. Your hacker probably understands you better than you understand him--and when he shares jokes with you, he's giving you a chance to see something special. If you feel brave, you might even ask him to explain some of them.

But don't be bothered when he tells you jokes that take a while to explain. Some of them are quite interesting.

5.4: My hacker counts from zero.

So does the computer. You can hide it, but computers count from zero. Most hackers do by habit, also.

Section 6: Is there anything else I should know?

6.1: I've found this document to be tremendously helpful. Is there anything I can do to say thank-you?

Wonderful of you to ask, and you certainly can. There are two authors who've contributed to this document, an original and a revision author. Both would appreciate cash donations (e-mail the original/revision authors for details). **The revision author would be very happy to receive a link to his home page: JonathansCorner.com (Browse around and see what he has to offer!)**

If you'd like to give something to one of the authors, but don't know which, why not flip a coin?

6.2: Are there any books that will help me understand my hacker?

Excellent question. Yes, there are. The following list is suggested:

- Please Understand Me or Please Understand Me II

What I said above about common manager/hacker differences was drawn from *Please Understand Me* as well as experience. Most hackers are *intuitive thinking* types, while managers who are confused by hackers tend to be *sensate judging* types. If you're in a hurry, buy *Please Understand Me* and read the descriptions for sensate judging and intuitive thinking types. You may find them tremendously helpful in understanding hackers. I've found them tremendously helpful in understanding managers.

Please Understand Me came out in the 1970s and describes what people are like. *Please Understand Me II* came out in the 1990s and describes both what people are like and what they can do. (It's about twice as long.) I prefer *Please Understand Me*.

- The New Hacker's Dictionary

Read the introduction and appendices; they're worth their weight in gold. Then read a definition a day--you'll learn a lot. This book is probably the #1 hacker classic, and provides an invaluable asset into understanding hacker thought. Don't worry if parts of it are hard to understand--you'll still learn something, and your hacker can probably explain the harder parts.

- Stranger in a Strange Land

Stranger in a Strange Land is a classic novel about a person who is raised by Martians and is brought to earth, a Martian mind in the body of a young man. There are not any hackers in this story, but if you can understand the protagonist in this story, you may find it much easier to understand and appreciate your hacker. Think of it as driving an automatic after you've learned to drive a stick.

- Guiding the Gifted Child

This award-winning title is a very practical book because it conveys understanding. It does a good enough job of it to be useful to several different kinds of people. It will help you understand the sort of people who become hackers.

This also is the only book on this list specifically intended to help people guide hacker-like people.

- The Cathedral and the Bazaar

Perhaps this has happened already. Or perhaps it will happen any day.

You try to reason with your hacker, and say, "Windows was made by the heavily funded efforts of a major corporation. Linux was made by some programmers on their spare time, and you can get it for free. Is Linux *really* as good as Windows?"

Your hacker rolls his eyes, appears to be counting to ten, gives you a very dirty look, and slowly says, "Is the upcoming band performance next door--live, in concert--*really* as good as this scratched-up CD?"

Your hacker believes that open source software is normally better than MicroSoft, and has very good reason to do so. This book explains why--and it may help you to get better software for less money, and put your business in a more competitive position. As far as hacker culture goes, it only illuminates a small part, but it does so very well.

Unfortunately, none of these books was specifically written to explain hacker culture to non-hackers. Fortunately, your hacker can help you connect the dots and put things together. Just ask him!

6.3: Has this FAQ been published?

The original version, in some form, has been bought by IBM DeveloperWorks, which funded part of the work. You could read their version (nicely edited) by following *this link* (non-functional as of 12/31/01; I've contacted IBM requesting a current URL and am waiting to hear back). IBM has also bought another article, the *Manager FAQ*, a guide to managers for hackers who are frustrated and confused by corporate life. The original author is justifiably happy with his work.

What's the copyright status on this? Can I make copies and share it with a friend who's confused by his hacker?

You may distribute as many copies of this document as you want. The original FAQ has the following notice:

This document is copyright 1995, 1996, 1998, 1999 Peter Seebach. Unaltered distribution is permitted.

When I let the original author know I was interested in a revision, and asked what the copyright status was, he said it was covered by the Artistic License. All changes in this revision are also covered by the Artistic License, all added material copyright 2001 by Jonathan Hayward. Distribute freely.

What's the author's e-mail, and what's the official distribution site

The original is officially distributed at *http://www.plethora.net/~seebs/faqs/hacker.html* by seebs@plethora.net, and the revision is at http://JonathansCorner.com/writing/hacker/ by author@cjshayward.com.

Are there any people the revision author would like to thank?

Yes. Jonathan Hayward would very much like to thank the original author, Peter Seebach, for writing an excellent FAQ and for giving him permission to modify it.

Any disclaimers?

DISCLAIMER: Both authors are hackers. Bias is inevitable.

Revision 1.0--Last modified April 3, 2008.

Why Study Mathematics?

One question which is raised by many people is, "Why should I study mathematics?". The question is usually asked from a perspective that there is probably no good and desirable reason for the speaker to study mathematics, but he will tolerate the minimum required because he has to, and then get on to more valuable and important things.

I readily acknowledge that there are many math classes which are drudgery and a general waste of time, and that many people have had experiences with mathematics which give them good reason to hold a distaste for the discipline. However, it is my hope that I may provide readers with an insight that there is something more to mathematics, and that this something more may be worthwhile.

Let's begin by looking at the reasons that the reader may already have come across for why he should study mathematics:

- There are certain basic computational skills that are needed in life. People should be able to figure out whether a 24-pack of their favorite soda for $3.89 is a better or worse deal than a 12-pack for $1.99.
- It builds character. I suffered through mathematics for such-and-such many years. So should you.

Of course, nobody explicitly says the second reason, but it may very well seem that way--like one of the hush-hushed truths that the Adult Conspiracy hides from students the same way it hides the fact that there is no Santa Claus from little children. And the first reason is something that many non-mathematical administrators believe.

But those are not the real reasons that a mathematician will give for why a nonmathematician should study mathematics, and what kind of mathematics a nonmathematician should study.

The first question which should be addressed is, "What is mathematics really about?"

The answer which many nonmathematicians may have is something along the lines of, "Mathematics, at its heart, is about learning and using formulas and things like that. In gradeschool, you learn the formulas and methods to add, subtract, multiply, and divide; then in middle school and high school it is on to bigger and better formulas, like the formula for the slope of a line passing through two points. Then in college, if your discipline unfortunately requires a little mathematics (such as the social sciences requiring statistics), you learn formulas that are even more complicated and harder to remember. The deeper you go into mathematics, the more formulas and rote methods you have to learn, and the worse it gets."

The best response I can think of to that question is to respond by analogy, and my response is along the following lines:

A child is in school will be taught various grammatical rules, sentence diagramming, and so on. These will be drilled and studied for quite a long while, and it must be said that this is not the most interesting of areas to study.

An English teacher who is asked, "Is this what your discipline is really about?", will almost certainly answer, "No!". Perhaps the English student is proficient in grammar, but that's not what English is about. English is about literature--about stories, about ideas, about characters, about plots, about poetic description, about philosophy, about theology, about thinking, about life. Grammar is not studied so that people can suffer through learning more pointless grammar; grammar is studied to provide students with a basic foundation from which they will be able to use the English language. It is a little drudgery which is worked through so that students may behold an object of great beauty.

This is the function of the formulas and rules of mathematics. Not rules and formulas so that the student is prepared for more rules and formulas, but rules and formulas which are studied so that the student can go past them to see what mathematics is really about.

And what is mathematics really about? Before I give a full answer, let me say that it is something like what English is about.

The one real glimpse that someone who has been through high school may have had of mathematics is in the study of geometry. There are a few things about high school geometry that I would like to point out:

- In geometry, one is given certain axioms and postulates (for example, the parallel postulate--given a line and a point not on the line, there is exactly one line through the given point which does not intersect the given line), definitions (a circle is the set of points equidistant (at an equal distance) from a given point), and undefined terms (point, line). From those axioms and postulates, definitions, and undefined terms, one begins to explore what they imply--theorems and lemmas.
- In geometry, rote memorization is not enough--and, in fact, is in and of itself one of the least effective approaches to take. It is necessary to understand--to get an intuitive grasp of the material. Learning comes from the "Aha!" when something clicks and fits together--then it is the idea that remains in the student's memory.
- Geometry builds upon itself. One starts with fundamentals (axioms, postulates, definitions, and undefined terms), and uses them to prove basic theorems, which are in turn used along with axioms and postulates to prove more elaborate theorems, and so on. It is like a building--once the foundation has been laid, beams and walls may be secured to the foundation, and then one may continue to build up

from the foundation and from what has been secured to the foundation. Geometry is an edifice built on its fundamentals with logic, and the structure that is ultimately built is quite impressive.

- Geometry is an abstract and rigorous way of thinking. (More will be made of this later.)
- Geometry is about creative problem solving. The aforespoken edifice--or, more specifically, what is in that edifice--is used by the geometer as tools with which to solve problems. Problem solving--figuring out how to prove a theorem or do a construction (which is a special kind of theorem)--is a creative endeavor, as much as painting, musical improvisation, or writing (and I am writing as one who does mathematics, paints, improvises, and writes).

Imagine a dream where there are many pillars--some low, some high--all of which are too high to step up to, and all of which are wide enough to stand upon.

Now imagine someone dreaming this dream. That person looks at one of the pillars and asks, "Has anyone been on top of that pillar?" Then one of the Inhabitants of his dream answers, "No, nobody has been on top of that pillar." Then the person looks at another of the pillars, which has a set of stairs next to it, and asks, "Has anyone been on top of that pillar over there?". The answer is, "Yes, someone has, and has left behind a set of steps. You may take those steps and climb up on top of the pillar yourself, if you wish."

And this person continues, and sees more pillars. Some of them stand alone, too high to step up to, and nobody has been to those. Others have had someone on top, and there is always a set of steps which the person left behind, by which he may climb up personally. And the steps go every which way--some go straight up, some go one way and then another, some seem to almost go sideways. Some are very strange. Some pillars have more than one set of steps. But all of them lead up to the top of the pillar.

The person dreaming may well have the impression that one

gets atop a pillar by laying down one step, then another, then another, until one has assembled steps that reach to the top of the pillar. And, indeed, it is possible to climb the steps up to the pillars that others have gone to first.

But that impression is wrong.

And the person sees what really happens when the guide becomes very excited and says, "Look over there! There is a great athlete who is going to attempt a pillar that nobody has ever been atop!"

And the athlete runs, and jumps, and sails through the air, and lands on top of the pillar.

And when the athlete lands, there appears a set of stairs around the pillar. The athlete climbs up and down the stairs a few times to tidy them up for other people, but the stairs were produced, not by laying down slabs of stone one atop another, but by jumping.

Then the guide explained to the dreamer that the athlete had learned to jump not only by looking at the steps that others had left, but by jumping to other pillars that already had steps, instead of using the steps.

Then the dreamer woke up.

What does the story mean?

The pillars are mathematical facts, some proven and some unproven.

The pillars that stand alone are mathematical facts that nobody has proven.

The pillars that stand with steps leading up to them are mathematical facts that have been proven.

The steps are the steps of proofs, the little assertions. As some of the steps are bizarre, so are some proofs. As some pillars have more than one path of steps, so some facts have more than one known proof.

The leap is a flash of intuition, by which the mathematician knows which of many steps will take him where he wants to go.

As the steps appeared when the leap was made, so the proof appears when the flash of intuition comes. The athlete then tidied up the steps, as the mathematician writes down and clarifies the proof, but the proof comes from jumping, not from building one step on another.

The athlete was the mathematician.

Finally, the athlete became an athlete not only by climbing up and down existing steps, but also by jumping up to pillars that already had steps--one becomes skilled at making intuitive leaps, not only by learning existing proofs, but also by solving already proven problems as if there were no proof to read.

As one philosophy major commented to me, "Mathematicians *do* proofs, but they don't *use* them."

That flash of insight is the flash of inspiration that artists work under, and in this sense a mathematician is very similar to an artist. (What do a mathematician and an artist have in common? Both are pursuing beauty, to start with...)

This character of mathematics that is captured in geometry is true to geometry, but the actual form that it takes is largely irrelevant. Other branches of mathematics, properly taught, could accomplish just the same purpose, and for that matter could just as well replace geometry. Two other disciplines which draw heavily on applied mathematics, namely computer science and physics, have essentially the same strong points. I would hold no objections, for that matter, if high school geometry classes were replaced by strategy games like chess and go.

Mathematics is about puzzle solving; I would refer the reader to works such as Raymond Smullyan's *The Lady or the Tiger?* and Colin Adams's *The Knot Book: an Elementary Introduction to the Mathematical theory of Knots*. There are many people to whom mathematics is a recreation, consisting of the pleasure of solving puzzles. If mathematics is approached as memorizing incomprehensible formulas and hoping to have the good luck to guess the right formula at the right time, it will be a chore and a torture. If it is instead approached as puzzle solving, the activity will yield unexpected pleasure.

My father has a doctorate in physics and teaches computer science. He has said, more than once, that he would like for all of his students to take physics before taking his classes. There is a very important and simple reason for this. It is not because he wants his students to program physics simulators, or because there is any direct application of the mathematics in physics to the computer science he teaches. There isn't. It is because of the problem solving, the manner of thinking. It is because someone who has learned how to think in a way that is effective in physics, will be able to think in a way that is effective in computer science.

This applies to other disciplines as well. Ancient Greek philosophers, and medieval European theologians, made the study of geometry a prerequisite to the study of their respective disciplines. It was not because the constructions or theorems would be directly useful in making claims about the nature of God. Like physics and computer science, there was no direct application. But in order to study geometry, one had to be able to think rigorously, analytically, critically, logically, and abstractly.

Thinking logically and abstractly is an important discipline in life and in other academic disciplines that consist of thinking--it has been said that if you can do mathematics, you can do almost anything. The main reason mathematics is valuable to the non-mathematician is as a form of weight lifting for the mind. Even when the knowledge has no application, the finesse that's learned can be useful.

To the non-mathematician, mathematics is a valuable discipline which offers practice in how to think well--both analytic thought and problem solving. Mathematics classes will most profitably be approached, not as "What is the formula I have to memorize," but with ideas such as those enumerated here. The nonmathematician who approaches a mathematics class as an opportunity for disciplined thought and problem solving will do better, profit more, and maybe, just maybe, enjoy the course.

It is my the hope that this essay have provided the nonmathematician with an inkling of why it is profitable for people who aren't going to be mathematicians to still study mathematics.

Hayward's Unabridged Dictionary

Preface

Ambrose Bierce has created a most useful dictionary, serving the ever important function of drawing attention to that which people learn to ignore. I do not agree with all of what he says, but none the less consider it immensely valuable. It is my opinion that subtlety and wit are entirely too scarce. Sometimes this work is a bit caustic; unfortunately, gently worded points are often gently ignored. Bierce wrote that his work was addressed to people who "prefer dry wines to sweet, sense to sentiment, wit to humor and clean English to slang." This work is written preferring subtlety and allusion to the blatant, thought to convenience, and honesty to comfort.

I would not be entirely honest to claim that this work is entirely my own. Some of the ideas are bits and pieces I've picked up here and there; I have done the work of a compiler as well of that of an author. The writing style is, to some effect, borrowed. And, of course, the actual idea for such a dictionary is not originally my own.

The definitions and aim are mostly theological, but occasionally dealing with some of the less agreeable aspects of American life. With apologies to Andy Rooney, there's probably something in here to offend anybody. I am not trying to cause a sting for the sake of causing a sting; rather, my hope in writing this is to be as the gadfly whom the Greek philosophers spoke of, with a sting that stirs people to thought and action. Where I point out problems, I believe that better is possible.

I could babble on for a few more pages, but it is my opinion that a frame does best not to be terribly gaudy and detract from the painting it holds. I believe that I've said enough, and that these definitions will introduce themselves.

Abortion Rights Opponent, *n.* The politically correct term for a person who holds and acts upon the conviction that an unborn child has at least a few rights which should be legally protected, notably the right not to be killed.

Accuse, *v.* To draw attention to another's similarity to oneself.

Accusatory, *adj*. Defensive.

Acting, *n.* A profession as different from politics as night is from day.

A member of the one profession puts on costumes and makeup, goes before cameras, dramatically reads lines written by someone else, and pretends to be someone that he isn't, providing unconvincing but amusing entertainment to millions.

A member of the other profession makes movies.

Administration, *n.* That body which is in charge of an organization, overseeing everything from personnel to organization to allocation of resources to wasting subordinates' time in meetings. The administration cares for the needs of the organization, placing those needs second only to its own needs, desires, and conveniences.

Administratium, *n.* A chemical element which makes plutonium look tame.

From the news release:

NEW CHEMICAL ELEMENT DISCOVERED

The heaviest element known to science was recently discovered by investigators at a major U.S. research university. The element, tentatively named administratium, has no protons or electrons and thus has an atomic number of 0. However, it does have one neutron, 125 assistant neutrons, 75 vice neutrons and 111 assistant vice neutrons, which gives it an atomic mass of 312. These 312 particles are held together by a force that involves the continuous exchange of meson-like particles called morons.

Since it has no electrons, administratium is inert. However, it can be detected chemically as it impedes every reaction it comes in contact with. According to the discoverers, a minute amount of administratium causes one reaction to take over four days to complete when it would have normally occurred in less than a second.

Administratium has a normal half-life of approximately three years, at which time it does not decay, but instead undergoes a reorganization in which assistant neutrons, vice neutrons and assistant vice neutrons exchange places. Some studies have shown that the atomic mass actually increases after each reorganization.

Research at other laboratories indicates that administratium occurs naturally in the atmosphere. It tends to concentrate at certain points such as government agencies, large corporations, and universities. It can usually be found in the newest, best appointed, and best maintained buildings.

Scientists point out that administratium is known to be toxic at any level of concentration and can easily destroy any productive reaction where it is allowed to accumulate. Attempts are being made to determine how administratium can be controlled to prevent irreversible damage, but results to date are not promising.

-Unknown

Admirable, *adj*. Embodying a virtue for whose absence the speaker excuses himself.

Adult Bookstore, *n*. A store offering books and movies which cater to infantile fantasies.

Advertising, *n*. (1) The fine art of lying to consumers about what is actually being sold. (2) A notable amendment of capitalist theory, whereby the market comes to favor, not the producers who sell the best product, but those who sell the best image. (3) A substantial misallocation of economic resources, whereby a tremendous portion of the economy which could do something useful, is wasted. (This misfortune has the additional demerit of providing a substantial competitive edge to those who use it.) For example, for each packet of mixed vegetables sold at the supermarket, more money is spent to place a colored picture on the packet than actually goes to the farmer. (4) ...

AI, *n*. Artificial Intelligence. A form of artificially generated computer intelligence which has proved remarkably successful at tasks such as playing chess as well as a grandmaster, using integral calculus to solve problems, and examining blood test results to diagnose blood disorders more accurately than most doctors, and which has utterly failed at tasks such as answering rudimentary questions about the story told in an I Can Read Book.

Allegory, *n.* A song whose content we find far too embarassing to believe could actually be a part of Holy Scripture.

Alternate, *adj*. Unacceptable, but shielded by the aegis of political correctness.

America, *n.* A great nation which like a melting pot; many ingredients come together in turbulent seething, those on the bottom get burned, and the scum rise to the top.

American Catholic, *n.* A conflation of 'American' and 'Catholic' in which 'American' takes precedence to 'Catholic'.

Amplified Bible, *n.* A new concept in translation theory, consisting largely of a word study crammed into a literal translation, listing possible meanings of words regardless of context. Thus the salad bar theologian is permitted to pick and choose the wording which will most emphatically support his point. Moreover, it avoids confusion by bracketed insertions, explaining what the author of the text failed to state clearly. Hence Mark 14:23 giving account of Jesus's actions at the Last Supper, says, "He also took a cup [of juice of grapes]..."

Anglicanism, *n.* See *Catholic Lite*.

Annoying, *adj*. Popular among companies who wish to persuade you to purchase their goods or services.

Annulment, *n.* The form of divorce practiced by those who classify divorce as mortal sin.

Anti-Realism, *n*. Any one of a number of philosophical systems whose proponents believe themselves to have established the nature of knowledge and reality to be such that it is impossible to make any definitive statements about the nature of reality.

Apocryphal, *adj*. Hidden.

Originally, the term denoted the writings of certain mystery religions which were hidden from all who were not part of the elite of initiates, such as the Orthodox Book of Common Prayer. Over time, the word has shifted in meaning. It is the nature of Christianity to proclaim its truths, not to hide them; thus, there was no need for apocryphal books in the first sense. The term was applied to books which were hidden for another, entirely different, reason; namely, books which were excluded due to heretical content, such as James or the book of Ecclesiastes. There may be a second connection between the two usages of the word, but it is wisely left unmentioned.

Appearance of Evil, *n*. A bane which people will commit evil in order to avoid.

Archaic, *adj*. Reflecting the best and most enduring relics of centuries gone before. Said of practices, ideas, and language which reflect a belief that wisdom may be found in thoughts of the past as well as those of the present. A pejorative term.

Arminianism, *adj*. The school of thought opposite Calvinism. Named after Arminius, a theologian who was taught under Calvin's successor, Theodore Beza. Arminius began to depart from Calvin's doctrine by teaching conditional predestination, as contrasted to Beza, who emphatically taught limited atonement.

Arranged marriage, *n*. A marriage not chosen by the parties involved; arranged marriages exhibit far lower divorce rates than those voluntarily chosen.

That they be more successful is not really as strange as it may seem at first.

> In America, you marry the girl you love; in India, you love the girl you marry.
>
> -A man speaking in a video on Indian philosophy

There is a fundamental difference in how arranged and voluntarily chosen marriages tend to be approached. Voluntary marriages tend to be approached as "If I can just find the right person, we can live happily ever after."; arranged marriages are not approached with any delusions of being an effortless bliss or some sort of box that one can take things out of without putting anything into. But with poorer conditions -- with a bride and groom that not only have not chosen each other, but have not necessarily met before the day of the wedding -- people decide to make it work. Therefore it is not the lands of arranged marriages, but America, which is the land of divorce.

The difference between expecting something to be fruitful without any effort and without any sacrifice, and expecting something to be difficult (but choosing via effort and sacrifice to make it work) is a difference between disappointment and a rewarding joy, and applies to much more of life than only marriage.

Aspirin, *n.* A drug used in the treatment of arthritis, commonly found in a container with a childproof cap.

Atheism, *n.* A religion requiring exceptional faith.

Attention Span, *n.* The length of time for which a person is able to maintain concentration. In most nations, a long attention span is valued as enabling understanding of well-developped, coherent, and complete arguments; in America,

Automobile, *n.* A transportation device hailed as the solution to the problem of providing transit without creating the pollution generated by a horse.

AV, *n.* Authorized Version. The Authorized Version, also known as the King James Version, is the original form of the Word of God. All subsequent paraphrases, while easier to read, are merely the word of man.

Bachelor's Degree, *n.* The primary degree offered by colleges attended as happy hunting grounds, such as Moody Bridal Institute.

Ballista, *n.* A device useful in the adjustment of sound systems playing elevator music.

Beatitude, *n.* A genre of didactic statement, used in the Sermon on the Mount.

> Blessed are the ticklish,
> for the touch of a friend shall fill them with laughter.
>
> -The Unauthorized Version

Beautiful, *adj.* Distorted and unnatural.

One of the enduring aspects of human culture is a tradition which universally establishes a single standard of beauty, one for the male body and (especially) one for the female.

There is some feature which may be attractive, and is exaggerated out of all proportion. Or, alternately, some feature which is unattractive, and is exaggerated out of all proportion.

Because a long and slender neck looks beautiful, a nice contrast to the thick bulges of a man's shape, there's a tribe in Africa which uses copper braces to stretch out women's necks to be a foot long.

China, noting that men have big feet and a feminine shape involves small feet, has the practice of footbinding, using the one kind of footwear tighter than climbing boots in order to painfully keep feet from growing any larger than those of a little girl.

Recent anthropological findings report an obscure culture which has successfully made the transition from ridiculous to bombastic. It has decided that the roundness of feminine beauty should be replaced with the shape of a pre-pubescent boy, and reacted to modern technology by using the woman's body as a repository for gelatinous capsules.

Beer Commercial, *n.* The *reductio ad disgustum* of advertising's image of women.

Bible, *n.* A work high on the tolerant people's list of books to be burned.

> We live in a pluralistic, multicultural society where young people raised according to the tenets of Hinduisn, Islam, or the humanist philosophy of Bertrand Russel must feel as welcome as young people raised on the Bible. Our solution to this challenge is ingenious. Knowing that the vast majority of young people are profoundly ignorant of the Bhagavad Gita, or of the Koran, or for that matter of the philosophy of Bertrand Russel, we have decided in the interests of tolerance and pluralism to leave them equally ignorant of the Bible. Our young

people enjoy a perfect democracy of ignorance.

-Literary critic Peter Marchand, commenting on the removal of the Bible from public school classrooms

Billboard, *n*. An eyesore which possesses the additional demerit of being a distraction to drivers.

Drivers who take their eyes off the road to read billboards should make sure that they're sufficiently insured.

Just a thought.

-A billboard seen in Holland, Michigan

I think I shall never see
a billboard lovely as a tree.
Perhaps, unless the billboards fall
I shall never see a tree at all.

-Ogden Nash

Blind, *adj*. Possessing eyes that do not see. The prophet Isaiah spoke of people having eyes that do not see and ears that do not hear. That prophecy has had numerous fulfillments; of chief contemporary relevance is current underinterpretation of Biblical teachings on wealth.

Bombastic, *adj*. Of, from, or pertaining to the PC-USA.

Boot, *n*. An ingenious device used to keep astronauts on the moon from floating away in space.

Brainwashing, *n*. A cold Big Brother's constant barrage of propoganda to people under his thumb.

> One American who recently visited the People's Republic of China said that at first he wondered how people could tolerate the constant barrage of slogans on walls and radio telling everybody what to think. Then he realized that his own society reels under nonstop messages just as inane.
>
> -Doris Janses, *Living More with Less*, on
>
> advertising

Budweiser, *n.* A headache in a bottle. The dog of beers.

> With most beers, if you drink too much, you get a headache the day after. With Annheiser-Busch, you get a headache as you drink it.
>
> -A German student, spring '95

Bumber Sticker, *n.* A tool to present the ludicrous as unassailable. One bumber sticker, for instance, reads:

> PRO-CHOICE, PRO-CHILD
> EVERY CHILD A WANTED CHILD

This form of deep compassion is perhaps inspired by satirist fantasy author Terry Pratchett:

> Give a man a fire and keep him warm for a day. Light a man on fire and he will be warm for rest of his life.

Busy Signal, *n.* An elegant sound designed to prepare the ear to listen to country and western.

Cafeteria, *n.* A refectory instrumental in the building of fine and upstanding young students. The meat builds muscle, the milk builds bones, and the rest builds character.

> Friend: We're going to the cafeteria for dinner. Wanna come along?
>
> Student: Sorry, but I'm trying not to lose weight.

Canada, *n.* See *Northern Wastes.*

Canadian, *adj.* and *n.* An anti-American American.

Capital Punishment, *n.* A form of sentence found in the most dangerous of first world nations, used by the government to intimidate criminals who have been taught that violence is the way to solve their problems.

Category Mistake, *n.* An assumption embodied in an inappropriate question, inquiring about an undefined attribute, such as, "Is yellow square or round?", "Is the doctrine of the Trinity calm or excited?", or "What was the point of that speech?"

Catholic University, *n.* An academic environment where Orthodox are warmly invited on the theory that the Church must breathe mustard gas with both lungs.

Causality, *n.* The mechanism by which cause brings about effect, thoughtfully provided as a reminder to philosophers of who is in Heaven and who is on earth. The latter have responded by deciding under what bounds the former is permitted to operate.

CD, *n.* Compact Disc. Used to record musical works in accordance with the popular taste, the compact disc is a small, round plate made out of the same material as bulletproof windows. This is believed to be in anticipation of more sophisticated reactions to the material they contain.

Ceremonial Law, *n.* As established in the Pentateuch, an elaborate system of rules and regulations. Ceremonial law contained, of course, exacting detail governing the administration of rites and ceremonies, but also contained an intricate calendar of holy days, told which foods were clean and unclean, talked about objects which were consecrated and objects which were profane, described what haircuts were and weren't acceptable, and so on. Paul spoke of this in many places; in his epistle to the Colossians, he describes all of these things as shadows of the reality found in Christ. Christ nailed it to the cross, and the Church has raised it from the dead.

Chalice, *n.* A vessel used to hold drinks, which were sometimes augmented by various poisons.

> Lady Aster (to Churchill): Winston Churchill, if I were your wife, I would put poison in your cup.
>
> Churchill: Lady Aster, if you were my wife, I would drink it.

Chaotic, *adj.* Embodying chaos; uncontrolled and unpredictable. A chaotic situation is one in which presence of mind is good and absence of body is better.

Checks-and-balances, *n.* A system of government with power divided between different branches, so that no one man or branch can hold too much power. This is accomplished by providing each branch with "checks" on the power of others, to maintain a "balance", in order that (once the government has grown sufficiently corrupt) the amount of good that one honest man can inflict is kept within tolerable bounds.

Cheese, *n.* The most important ingredient in good pizza and successful television programming.

Childproof Cap, *n.* A safety device preventing parents from opening certain containers without their children's assistance.

Chivalry, *n.* A time-honored code of conduct which, at a time when most men treated women as chattels, demanded as central to a man's honor that women be accorded deference, protection, and respect. Considered by modern feminism to be a bane.

Christian Contemporary Music, *n.* A genre of song designed primarily to impart sound teaching, such as the doctrine that we are sanctified by faith and not by good taste in music.

Christian Film, *n.* A mode of expressing Christian doctrine which uses the same essential communication strategy as hard-core pornography, in that the form of storytelling leaves nothing to the imagination but the plot.

Christian Science, *n.* A system of doctrines with a name carefully chosen, word by word, in honor of the accuracy with which it describes the world.

Christmas, *n.* A yearly holiday celebrating the coming of the chief Deity of Western civilization: Mammon.

Church, *n.* An early substitute for America and the GOP.

Circular Definition, *n.* A definition which is circular.

Civilization, *n.* The state of living where people abide in cities rather than roam planes, conferring a respect for the value of human life not found among savages.

Reporter (To Gandhi): Mr. Gandhi, what do you think of Western civilization?

Gandhi: I think it would be a good idea.

Classic, *n.* A work which everybody wants to have read but nobody wants to read.

Closed-Minded, *adj.* Possessing a mind which, like a pipe sealed on both ends, does not permit ideas to enter and leave. Contrasted with an open mind, which permits ideas to flow, like water through a pipe, entering and exiting without leaving any trace. There is perhaps a third prospect, of weighing and examining most ideas against a higher standard to grab firm hold of what is meritorious and worth keeping and reject what is twisted and mistaken, but this idea does not occur sufficiently often to merit its own word. Promoting open-mindedness is perhaps the single greatest achievement of current thought.

> If Jesus Christ were to come today, people would not crucify him. They would ask him to dinner, and hear what he had to say, and make fun of it.
>
> -Thomas Carlyle

Coconut, *n.* Positive proof that plant life has been affected by the Fall. See also: *Pistachio*, *Cashew*.

Coffeehouse, *n.* A location symbolic of the fake intellectual scene, where people sit over a cup of coffee and talk about how open-minded they think they are.

Coin, *n.* The smallest unit of currency. The coin generally bears something symbolic of the nature and perspective of the people who create it -- what they value, what they think of. The highest coin in the United States bears a picture of a human being; the highest coin in Canada bears the image of a loon.

Coincidence, *n.* In television, a kind of event that happens to happen as often as people need it to.

Collateral Damage, *n.* Blood that flows like a river.

Comedian, *n.* An entertainer possessing every faculty relevant to amusement save the ability to be funny.

Commentary, *n.* A multivolume explanation of the meaning of a book, chapter, or (occasionally) single verse, such as Ecclesiastes 6:11.

Commitment, *n.* [*N.B.: definition pending upon completion of a search for relationships which are not viewed as temporary and disposable*]

Committee, *n.* The divine model of speedy application of resources to the point of need.

> For God so loved the world, that he formed a committee, that whosoever attendeth on it should not perish, but have everlasting life in which to await a decision.
>
> -The Unauthorized Version

Common Sense, *n.* An exceedingly uncommon commodity.

Communist, *n.* One of the money changers Jesus drove out of the temple.

Company, *n.* The associations a person is seen with, as a reflection of character. Keeping good company is one area where many Christians have gone above and beyond the example of Christ.

Computer Error, *n.* The juxtaposition of at least two purely human errors, one of which is attributing the problem to the computer.

Congress, *n*. A body of men whose sole purpose in existence is to pile law upon law upon law.

The fundamental belief embodied in this philosophy is that a nation at peace with itself is ordered and held together, not by love and true religion, nor by honor and morality, nor even by a minimal attempt to act according to Confucious's simple words, "Do not do unto others what you would not have them do unto you," but rather by the brute force of edicts issued by the sovereign.

Therefore, when the nation was first formed, and not only did held together but actually built itself up by leaps and bounds, the legislators believed it their duty to create laws. When the nation's growth began to slow and problems to increase, the legislators believed it their duty to attempt to improve the situation by creating laws. And now, as the nation is crumbling, when it is common for a mere child to carry a .45 caliber handgun because he does not feel safe at school, it is by the force of tax laws hundreds of pages long and penal codes which the lawmakers themselves could not hope to read that the legislature seeks to stem the ever advancing tide of chaos.

> The greater the number of laws and enactments, the greater the number of thieves and robbers.
>
> -Lao Tzu, *Tao Te Ching*

Conscience, *n*. An early artifact formerly serving the purpose now fulfilled by harsh penalties assigned as punishment for getting caught.

Conspicuous, *adj*. Trying to act inconspicuous.

Consumer Oriented Services, *n.* Religion within the bounds of amusement.

This fundamental category mistake places church meetings not within the category of religious services designed to help people worship and grow, loving enough to give a gadfly's sting, but rather action-packed spectacles designed to attract people who are seeking amusement. Seminaries, far from warning against this, are actually promoting it.

This is, unfortunately, not a novelty. Like schools, and USA-TODAY, and so on and so forth, just one more segment of society in need of a swift kick in the pants from Neil Postman.

Copyright, *n.* A legal protection acquired for a piece of information, commonly used by the author or publisher of a book, program, et cetera, to secure benefit$ from its use. While it is possible to be more lenient in what a copyright permits, that option ranks to many as an extremely gnu concept. Most commonly, all rights are reserved. Without the express written consent of the owner, *n.* part of the work may be be reproduced, stored in a retrieval system, or transmitted, in any form or by any means, electronic, mechanical, photocopying, recording, or biological.

Corporate Ladder, *n.* An awe inspiring structure which reaches to the clouds and leans against the wrong building.

> By working hard for eight yours a day, you may get to be a boss and work hard for twelve hours a day.
>
> -Mark Twain

Crash Test, *n.* A simulated collision, used to prove the safety superiority of larger and heavier cars by showing that they provide partial protection in an accident that a more maneuverable car would be able to avoid.

Creativity, *n.* An attribute which is admired and praised in figures of the past.

Cult, *n.* An aberrant group whose bizarre practices deviate from what is established and considered normative. Etymologically, the word signifies worship.

Cybertechnology, *n.* Technology which enters into the body, such as an artificial heart or robotic arm.

At present, a surgeon has access to books upon books of procedures designed to restore function to a hand injured, and yet not one procedure designed to improve the function of a hand uninjured. Cybertechnology which is not remedial -- a replacement for a defective heart or severed limb being examples of remedial cybertechnology -- is essentially the property of science fiction writers, who allow all manner of incredible technology to enter the body.

The prime exception, if it is to be counted as such, is chemical. There exist drugs which exert special impact on the body. Most are used in medical fashion -- an antibiotic or some other such function -- but there are a few which act to improve the function of a person in health. It was observed that smoking cigarettes causes people to breathe more deeply. Realizing this, and understanding the importance of oxygen to a developping child, doctors advised pregnant women to smoke. There are many other drugs which bring a similar improvement. The use of cocaine is a wonderful way to deal with depression, and the use of massive amounts of anabolic steroids brings an unequalled boost to athletic prowess.

This present lexicographer looks with great anticipation to the day when the cybertechnology described in novels may become commonplace.

Dance, *n.* An activity of joy and celebration given numerous references in Scripture (none of which are negative), now considered by staunch Christians to be demonic if enjoyed in community.

Dark Sucker, *n.* Supposedly, an alternative understanding of a light source.

This jesting theory states that darkness is something which obscures vision; we are able to see when the darkness is sucked out. Eventually, the dark suckers become full of darkness and themselves become dark; this explains why incandescent bulbs, fluorescent tubes, and candles universally turn dark when they cease to function.

The theory was probably devised by an electrical engineer, who wanted to do something silly while taking a break from drawing circuit diagrams.

Dating, *n.* A sequence of miniature marriages, complete with miniature sex, ending in miniature divorces.

Democracy, *n.* [Gk. *demos*, people, *cratein*, to rule. No connection to the etymology of 'demon'] A Utopian form of government based on the twin assumptions that the majority will generally do what is noble, just, and true, and that mass persuasion techniques cannot be used to set aside good judgement.

> Man's capacity for justice makes democracy possible, but man's inclination to injustice makes democracy necessary.
>
> -Reinhold Niehbuhr

It has been said that television is an example of democracy at its ugliest; there is no accountability, and people tend to watch something other than what they would publicly be seen as associating with. It is a degenerating morass, increasingly portraying sexual sin as harmless and bloodshed as an amusing sport; recent years have seen the network television premiere of America's first made-for-TV war. It was wrong of the Evil Empire to define a just war as anything which advances the cause of communism; we know that a war is only justified if it makes the world safe for freedom and democracy. Were that war not to have been fought, Kuwaiti refugees would still be stranded in the surrounding nations' disco parlors. We would not have been able to restore the tyranny and human rights violations of the Kuwaiti ruling family, nor, more importantly, implement important alterations to the infrastructure of Baghdad to better deal with the problem of overpopulation. All of this is necessary to be able to listen to a child's shattered dreams, and then explain why Daddy isn't coming home.

For the majority to oppress the minority is perfectly democratic; the condition for democracy is the desire of the majority, a consideration independent of right and wrong. In perhaps the most spectacular debacle of all, Adolf Hitler rose to power in Germany, through means which can only be described as unimpeachably democratic.

> **Eloquence**, *n.* The art of persuading fools that white is the color that it appears to be. It includes the gift of making any color appear white.
>
> -Ambrose Bierce, The Devil's Dictionary.

Demon Rum, *n.* An unfortunate by-product of Jesus's first miracle.

Denomination, *n.* A group of schismatics whose conduct we find to be in accordance with Scripture.

Department of Defense, *n.* A Ministry of War continually involved in operations which have little or nothing to do with the integrity of national borders.

Deus Ex Machina, *n.* [Lat. *deus*, god, *ex*, out of; from, *machina*, machine] (1) In fiction, an unrealistic solution to a problem, which miraculously works. For example, a poor family's financial struggles finding resolution in the death of a hitherto unknown relative who willed them his wealthy estate. (2) In nonfiction, an unrealistic technological solution to a problem with its origin in the evil within the human heart, which miraculously fails. For example, infanticide on demand as a solution for the contempt for children which causes child abuse.

Dictator, *n.* An evil man who maintains power by intimidation and force, refusing to obey the United States.

Dinosaur, *n.* An immense prehistoric beast with a mental capacity lower than that of a field mouse. Figuratively, the term is used in a very pejorative manner by computer scientists, in reference to annoying machines which have miniscule capabilities and take inordinate amounts of time to do anything useful. Dinosaurs typically make obnoxious noises, and are bulky eyesores with glowing green against a somewhat darker but none the less nauseating background. For all the disagreeable things in American culture, we have learned the importance of teaching computer literacy to young children.

Disclaimer, *n.* A kind of publisher's preface accompanying books, advertisements, et cetera, for the edification of any lawyers who may happen to read the work. Most disclaimers are either patently false, as the disclaimer by cigarette manufacturers that colorful advertisements sporting cartoon characters are not meant to attract the attention of children, or blatantly obvious, as the following words found before many novels:

> This is a work of fiction. The characters and plot of this story are solely the product of the author's imagination. Any resemblance to the personality or actions of any person, living or dead, is purely coincidental.

Dishonesty, *n.* A condition which is considered a vice until it is channeled into the virtuous and proper bounds of tact.

Dispensationalism, *n.* Systematic theology as an excuse for lack of faith.

Divorce, *n.* A legalized form of child abuse.

DOS, *n.* Disk Operating System. A set of programs offering crude disk operations, frequently confused with a complete and robust operating system.

> A master was explaining the nature of Tao to one of his novices, "The Tao is embodied in all software -- no matter how insignificant," said the master.
>
> "Is the Tao in a hand-held calculator?" asked the novice.
>
> "It is." came the reply.
>
> "Is the Tao in a video game?"
>
> "The Tao is even in a video game," said the master.
>
> "And is the Tao in the DOS for a personal computer?"
>
> The master coughed and shifted his position slightly.

"The lesson is over for today."

-Geoffrey James, The Tao of Programming, 4.3

Doubt, *n.* The cornerstone of the four cardinal virtues of classical modernity.

DoxaSoma, *n.* The Christian spiritual practice of meditative prayer through exercise, balance, and body posture. (Minimum 85% recycled from Hindu spiritual practices.)

Driver's License, *n.* A form of identification required in order to legally purchase alcoholic beverages.

Dystopia, *n.* Utopian theory in practice.

Easter, *n.* The highest point of the Christian calendar, named after the Babylonian whore goddess.

Edifice, *n.* A building antedating the advent of the Bauhaus aesthetic.

Educated, *adj.* Unemployed with a degree.

Education Party, *n.* The party which nominated for important office a man lacking sufficient training to spell personal names or those of common household items.

Eh?, *tic.* See *Like.*

Eighteen, *n.* In the eyes of the United States government, the number of years which constitute the age of accountability. At this age, a person is no longer treated as a child, but as a mature adult with sound judgment. Eighteen years is old enough to give a signature that bears legal weight without the approval of a legal guardian, old enough to decide the fate of a human life or nation by serving as a juror on a capital case or by casting a vote, old enough to enlist or be conscripted to military service, old enough to kill enemy soldiers and old enough to die in combat, but too young and immature to visit a restaurant and enjoy a glass of wine with dinner.

Eisegesis, *n.* Reading one's meaning into a text, as distinguished from exegesis, drawing the meaning out of a text. It is interesting to note that the people most skilled in eisegesis, particularly as it pertains to Scripture, do not generally understand the distinction.

Electricity, *n.* A modern convenience which, when combined with running water, is capable of making life very inconvenient.

Element, *n.* The basic building blocks of which all matter is built. According to the ancient Greeks, there were four elements: Earth, Air, Fire, and Water. Science has progressed beyond that; matter generally consists of atoms, the ultimate, indivisible unit. Atoms in turn are built of more fundamental and elementary particles, and the elementary particles combine in various ways to generate the forms of matter we know of -- Solid, Liquid, Gas, and Plasma.

Embarrassment, *n.* The one fly in the ointment that it is hoped that opponents won't notice. In general, attempts are made to discredit embarrassments, the results of which can frequently be very amusing to watch. Fortunately, there is an exception if the embarrassment comes from Scripture. Holy Scripture is recognized to be God-breathed, and any embarrassing passage is taken very seriously; exegetes attempt to discern the passage's true meaning through careful reading and detailed word studies.

> Man will occasionally stumble over the truth, but most of the time he will pick himself up and continue

on.

-Winston Churchill

Enlightenment, *n.* The beginning of the fall of Western civilization and thought.

Environmentalist, *n.* One devoted to a particular political agenda, regardless of its impact on the environment.

A recent project at Argonne National Laboratory was working on a new generation of nuclear reactor which would be in many ways a dream come true. Its design would be such that meltdown would be physically impossible. It could run on nuclear waste from other plants, not only generating power but reducing them to material which would become harmless in a matter of roughly a century, rather than millions of years. It could run on nuclear warheads, thus not only providing a safe and permanent manner to dispose of some of the most appalling and destructive devices ever created, but so doing in a manner which would provide useful energy to hospitals and families; a beautiful picture of what it means to beat swords into ploughshares.

However, it is still nuclear, and, in the eyes of environmentalism, all nuclear power is evil and must be stopped at any cost. This project was, most definitely, stopped at any cost. It was terminated at great monetary cost; it was nearing completion, and, now that it was ready to be tested on different materials, those materials must be disposed of, at a cost of ninety-four million dollars more than it would have cost to complete. It was terminated at great environmental cost; those materials are dangerous nuclear wastes, and, though they were going to be made harmless, they must now be disposed of in established manners; that is to say, function as the nuclear waste that environmentalists so adamantly oppose. However, they stopped something bearing the dirty 'n' word, so environmentalists are now happy.

It is at least fortunate that environmentalists do not yet have the means to extinguish the sun.

Episcopalianism, *n.* A most interesting combination of Catholic and Protestant, quite effectively combining the worst of both worlds.

Euphemasia, *n.* In writing, choice of words and phrases that skillfully dance around what they mean. This avoids offending people, and puts any alternative certainty of the work being taken seriously out of its state of being differently happy.

Evangelical, *n.* A believer who is devoted to the doctrine of Sola Scriptura and verse by verse study of Scripture. The Great Commission is at the center of their ethics, and they believe in proclaiming Christ by deed as well as word. Thus many of them wisely abide by prohibitions, against dangerous things such as the following: card games, drinking, dancing, movies, swearing... While none of these are technically outlawed by Scripture, they are thought to be good ideas entirely in accordance with its essential teaching, as reflected in verses such as the following: Ps. 149:3, Eccl. 9:7, II Cor. 4:6, Gal. 1:6-8, 3:1-2, 5:1, 12,18,22-25, Eph. 2:15, Col. 2:8,13-14,16,20-23, I Thes. 5:19, I Tim. 4:1-5.

Evil, *n.* That which is twisted, depraved, and wicked.

Once upon a time, a king wished that his people know what evil was, so that his people could learn to recognize and flee from it. He issued a summons, that, in a year, all of his artists should come to him with one picture, to show what was evil. The best picture would be displayed to the people.

In a year, they all appeared at the king's palace. There were very few artists in the kingdom, but those who were there were very skillful, and worked as they had never worked before. Each brought a picture beneath a shroud.

The king turned to the first artist who had come. "Jesse, unveil your picture, and tell us its interpretation."

Jesse lifted the cloth. Against a background of blackened skulls was a dark green serpent, the color of venom and poison, with eyes that glowed red. "Your Majesty, it was the Serpent whose treacherous venom deceived man to eat of the forbidden fruit. The eye is the lamp of the body, and the Serpent's eye burns with the fires of Hell. You see that beyond the Serpent are skulls. Evil ensnares unto death and outer darkness."

The court murmured its approval. The picture was striking, and spoke its lesson well. The king, also, approved. "Well done, Jesse. If another picture is chosen, it will not be because you have done poorly. Now, Gallio, please show us your work."

Gallio unveiled his painting. In it was a man, his face red and veins bulging from hate. In his hand, he held a curved dagger. He was slowly advancing towards a woman, cowering in fear. "Your Majesty, man is created in the image of God, and human life is sacred. Thus the way we are to love God is often by loving our neighbor. There are few blasphemies more unholy than murder. You have asked me for a picture to show what evil is, that your subjects may flee from it. This is evil to flee from."

The court again murmured its approval, and the king began to shift slightly. It was not, as some supposed, because of the repellent nature of the pictures, but because he had secretly hoped that there would be only one good picture.

Now, it was evident that the decision would not be so simple. "Gallio, you have also done well. And Simon, your picture?"

Simon unveiled his picture, and people later swore that they could smell a stench. There, in the picture, was the most hideous and misshapen beast they had ever seen. Its proportions were distorted, and its colors were ghastly. The left eye was green, and taller than it was wide. The right eye was even larger than the left, red, bloodshot, and flowing with blood; where there should have been a pupil, a claw grotesquely protruded. It was covered with claws, teeth, fur, scales, blood, slime, tentacles, and bits of rotted flesh; several members of the court excused themselves. "However it may be disguised, evil is that which is sick, distorted, and ugly."

There was a long silence. Finally, the king spoke again. "I see that there are three powerful pictures of evil, any one of which is easily a masterpiece and well fit to show to the people. Barak, I know that you have been given artistic genius, and that perhaps your picture will help me with this difficult decision. Unveil your picture."

Barak unveiled his picture, and an awestruck hush fell over the court. There, unveiled, was the most beautiful picture they had ever seen.

The picture was in the great vault of a room in a celestial palace. It was carved of diamond, emerald, ruby, jasper, amethyst, sardonyx, and chrysolite. Through the walls of gem, the stars shone brightly. But all of this was nothing, compared to the creature in the room.

He carried with him power and majesty. He looked something like a man, but bore glory beyond intense. His face shone like the sun blazing in full force, his eyes flashed like lightning, and his hair like radiant flame. He wore a robe that looked as if it had been woven from solid light. In his left hand was a luminous book, written in letters of gold, and in his right hand was a sharp, double edged sword, sheathed in fire and lightning.

The king was stunned. It took him a long time to find words, and then he shouted with all of his might.

"You fool! I ask you for a picture of evil, and you bring me this! It is true that fools rush in where angels fear to tread, and that, like unthinking beasts, they do not hesitate to slander the glorious ones. What do you have to say for yourself and for this picture? I shall have an explanation now, or I shall have your head!"

Barak looked up, a tear trickling down his cheek. "Your Majesty, do you not understand? It is a picture of Satan."

Exaggerate, *v.* In satire, to tell a frog, as if it were the present, a plausible description of what the water may be like in a few minutes.

Excuse, *n.* A statement which serves as evidence of a guilty conscience.

Explanation, *n.* An account of a situation which does not threaten the speaker's prejudice.

In George MacDonald's *The Princess and the Goblin*, princess Irene gets lost in her mountain home and finds a mysterious grandmother, who gives her a silver ring attached to an invisibly fine strand of spider-silk, and tells her that if she follows the thread Irene will find her grandmother's room. One time, Irene gets lost and follows the thread out of the house, in and out of all kinds of dark and unfamiliar caverns deep inside a goblin-infested mountain. She finds the imprisoned miner-boy Curdie and brings him to her grandmother. Curdie follows along, but cannot believe her strange account: even in the room where Irene claims to be speaking with her grandmother, Curdie sees only a dark and dirty garret. A bitter argument ensues, and Curdie returns home, vexed.

His mother coaxes the explanation out of him:

> Then Curdie made a clean breast of it, and told them everything.
>
> They all sat silent for some time, pondering the strange tale. At last Curdie's mother spoke.
>
> "You confess, my boy," she said, "there is something about the whole affair you do not understand?"
>
> "Yes, of course, mother," he answered. "I cannot understand how a child knowing nothing about the mountain, or even that I was shut up in it, should come all that way alone, straight to where I was; and then, after getting me out of the hole, lead me out of the mountain too, where I should not have known a step of the way if it had been as light as in the open air."
>
> "Then you have no right to say what she told you was not true. She did not take you out, and she must have had something to guide her: why not a thread as well as a rope, or anything else? There is something you cannot explain, and her explanation may be the right one."
>
> "It's no explanation at all, Mother; and I can't believe it. Darwinism is the only game in town."

Fallenness, *n*. The defining characteristic of the present human condition. C.S. Lewis spoke wisely:

> There are two types of people in this world:
> those who say to God, "Thy will be done,"
> and those to whom God says, "Thy will be done."

Herein may be found the explanation for most of human history.

Familiar, *adj*. Considered to be safe and good.

Fashion, *n*. The progressive self-revelation of the imago dei.

Fast, *n*. A New Testament practice which most current-day Christians have quickly disposed of.

Fast Food, *n*. An enterprise which pioneered the use of disposable polystyrene packaging, which was useful and convenient to the customer on the go. Now, due to consumer pressure, the fast food industry is genuinely concerned about the environment. The packaging presently used is biodegradable. The contents, unfortunately, are not.

Fat Free, *adj*. See *Taste Free*.

Feminism, *n*. Like most philosophical and ideological currents, truth gone mad.

Feminism at its heart embodies a substantial truth -- that women have historically been treated as second class citizens (if even that), and that no society can call itself just while conducting business as usual -- and its development tells many other truths: love, nurturance, and cooperation are foundational virtues in the life of a society; emotion is an integral part of being human; human relationships and community are important; pornography degrades women and children, and promotes rape; no means no.

However, both first wave feminism (which sought equality on existing terms) and second wave feminism (which seeks to completely redefine the terms of equality) make statements that, if carried to their logical conclusions, are absolute madness. (To which many feminists would reply that logic is a tool of male oppression.)

At the root of this is a failure to identify the moral structure of the universe as ordered by a God who is the ultimate of masculinity -- more Yang than Yang -- and a failure to recognize femininity as a created good which, by its very nature, does not and should not order the universe. First wave feminism did not understand the differences between masculine and feminism; the second wave sees all good in terms of the feminine and all evil in terms of the masculine.

Thus is embarked upon a project to remake society (which consists entirely of male oppression) into a world of feminine good. The results vary from the comedic to the destructive -- and end up to be at least as baneful to women as men.

To be swept away are all of the classics of literature and philosophy: their purpose is to justify the exploitation of women. Men's languages are to be replaced by feminine tongues; they revolve around logic rather than emotion, and are cruelly imposed on little girls before they can learn to communicate by their own natures. Never mind that women talk more than men, or that the study of languages is dominated by women. Our languages are oppressive. Newton's *Principia Mathematica*, the landmark work which laid out the foundations of calculus, is "Newton's rape manual."

Of course, nearly all movements have a lunatic fringe, but it is unnecessary to look at feminism's fringes to see the destructive. Many, many women are told to regard *every* man as a potential rapist. Trust is essential to every human relationship; it is a building block as foundational as love and honesty. Yet feminism believes it in the best interest of women to regard every moment with every man as potentially turning into one of the deepest and inhuman violations possible; this means that they are to spend every moment with every man in unending fear.

Furthermore, at least a certain form of feminism, like multiculturalism, relativism, etc. in that they form a core of orthodoxy which the herd of free thinkers is shocked and indignant to see someone go against. Never mind, for example, that early feminism and the present black womanist movement found and find abortion to be unacceptable; anyone who stands against the legality of abortion is an abortion rights foe (just imagine what would happen if anyone used language that loaded in reference to a liberal...) who stands in the way of what can only be seen as a woman's private rights over her own body. Never mind that other cultures -- even those which have had substantial impact from other peoples -- are not multicultural and do not see the multiplicity of existant cultures as suggesting that everything is arbitrary, no one way of thinking or acting to be preferred over any other; the existence of other cultures which see things differently is proof that everything is an arbitrary matter for which there can be no standard of judgement. (Never mind that there are a great many things, such as the Natural Law and the absence of our optimistic belief in human progress, which remain remarkably constant across various cultures and ages.) And relativism, of course, means relativism on some very specific points -- namely, everything that forms a part of this core of orthodoxy is something that no open-minded person could seriously question, and every belief which could substantially challenge the core of orthodoxy is a relative and subjective opinion which anybody may hold on condition that it is not actually believed to be true. Upon even a few minutes of inspection, it would appear that these beliefs are not only furnished by a zeal not matched by thought, but are not even internally consistent.

But all of this doesn't really matter, because feminism and its cousins are not meant to be thought about; only fought for.

With allies and a supporting movement like this, what woman needs enemies?

Filiopatros Clause, *n.* An exceedingly poor excuse for a schism.

Flag, *n.* See *Idol.*

Flashlight, *n.* An instrument of imperception which obscures vision by producing a concentrated glare at one point which is sufficiently intense to prevent the user from seeing anything else. Environmentalists have brought the cleverness of this device one step further by producing the solar powered flashlight.

Foetus, *n.* A very young child whom it is deemed expedient to consider to be otherwise.

Form, *n.* A piece of paper used as by administrations to deter people from using their services. It is the opinion of this lexicographer that the following form could be of the utmost assistance in helping bureaucracies more effectively serve those under their care.

Form to Request Information in the Form of a Form

Section 1: Personal Information

Name: ___________________________ **Sex:** [ ]M [ ]F **Date of Birth:** __/__/__
Social Security Number: ___-__-____
Driver's License Number: ____-____-____
VISA/MasterCard Number: ____-____-____-____
Mailing Address, Business:
Street:_____________________________
City:_______________ State:__ **ZIP Code:**_____
Mailing Address, Home:
Street:_____________________________
City:_______________ State:__ **ZIP Code:**_____
Telephone, Work: (___)___-____, Ext. ____
Telephone, Home: (___)___-____
Telephone, Car: (___)___-____
Beeper: (___)___-____ **Chicago High School:** [ ]Y [ ]N
E-mail Address:
____
_________ (if address is in domain aol.com or webtv.net, please explain on a separate sheet of paper)
Height: _', __" Weight: ___# Hair: ______ Eyes: _____ Blood type: __ IQ: __
Political Affiliation: [ ]Federalist [ ]Republican [ ] Democrat [ ]Libertarian [ ]Monarchist [ ]Socialist [ ]Marxist [ ]Communist [ ]Nazi [ ]Fascist [ ] Anarchist [ ]Other (Please specify:_____________)
Citizenship: [ ]United States, including Canada and other territories [ ]Mexico [ ]California [ ]Other (Please specify:____________________)
Race: [ ]Caucasian/Pigmentally Challenged [ ] African [ ]Asian [ ]Hispanic/Latino [ ]Amerindian [ ]Heinz-57 [ ]Other (Please specify: __________________) [ ]An athletic event where people run around an oval again and again and again.

Page 1 * End of Section 1 of 3

Section 2: Form Description

Length of Form, in Characters: _____
Number of Questions or Required Data: ____
Expected Time to Complete: __ Hours, __ Minutes, __ Seconds.
Expected Mental Effort Required to Complete: __________________________ (if form would insult the intelligence of a senile hamster, please explain on a separate sheet of paper)
Expected number of questions judged to be annoying, unnecessary, and/or personally offensive: __
Expected time wasted on questions judged to be annoying, unnecessary, and/or personally offensive: __ Hours, __ Minutes, __ Seconds.
Expected blood pressure increase while filling out form: __ mmHg systolic, __ mmHg diastolic.

If further contemplation has led you to believe that some of the questions asked are not strictly necessary to provide the service that you offer upon completion of said form, please enclose revised prototype here.

Page 2 * End of Section 2 of 3

Section 3: Essay Questions

Please explain, in 500 words or less, your philosophy concerning the use of forms.

Please explain, in 200 words or less, why you designed this form as you did.

Please explain, in 300 words or less, why you believe that this form is necessary. If you are in a service oriented sector and desire to require the form of people you serve, please explain why you believe that requiring people to fill out forms constitutes a service to them.

When this form is completed, please return to the address provided. The Committee for Selecting Forms will carefully examine your case and delegate responsibility to an appropriate subcommittee.

Please allow approximately six to eight weeks for the appointed subcommittee to lose your file in a paper shuffle.

Page 3 * End of Section 3 of 3

Formal Equivalent, *n*. The style of translation favored by those who hold the highest view of Scripture. The philosophy of formal equivalence justly realizes the secondary place the transmission of ideas, themes, and sagas holds to the importance of direct renderings of individual words and the preservation of the original word order. Even those who attempt to render thought for thought pay due homage to formal equivalence in their renderings of metaphors in that most highly respected of books, the Song of Songs.

FORTRAN, *n*. See *BASIC*.

Free, *adj*. Complimentary with your purchase of an item overpriced by more than the value of the gift.

Freedom, *n.* One of the foundational aspects of the Christian walk. Its proper understanding is one of the pivotal themes of Galatians, a book which refutes a heresy that shocked Paul so greatly that he skipped the usual pleasantries in beginning his letter. There are two major historical interpretations, both of which (in some form or other) can claim many orthodox adherents.

The first, the libertine interpretation, states that, due to grace and forgiveness, there are really no behaviors a Christian should avoid. Hence the believer is free to participate in orgies, free to have conduct dictated by an addiction, free to touch molten iron, and so on.

The second, the Judaizing interpretation, states that grace and forgiveness make sense only if there is such a thing as sin, and have an extensive list of sins to avoid. At the same time, the essence of their teaching is freedom. Hence the believer is free (at least one day in seven) to drop an article of clothing once every few steps, free to have conduct dictated by a written code of rules, free to become castrated, and so on.

Both of these emphasize freedom as the center of their walk. There is rumored to be a third interpretation, but it does not claim enough adherents to be worth explaining.

Gadfly, *n.* A sage who speaks with honesty which is universally appreciated and rewarded with unequalled travel opportunities.

Gang, *n.* A group of armed cowards found in major cities, fighting for control of streets and drug money, and intimidating and beating up whoever they think they can get away with, beating up whoever they don't like, and so on, as contrasted to the activities of the police department.

Garrotte, *n.* An early predecessor to the modern necktie.

Gay Theology, *n.* An abhorrent system of supposed interpretation, which serves only to excuse away the Word of God and abridge the moral requirements of the Gospel in order to permit a lifestyle which is a perversion of nature and a stench in God's nostrils, as contrasted to the beliefs and practices of good, prosperous, normal American Christians.

Gentleman, *n.* A man. The term embodies a degree of respect, and reflects a particular ideal of manhood.

Perhaps best summarized in the words, "A gentleman is a gentle man," this ideal did not hold that manhood was to be measured by the ability to carry a Gatling gun, demolish buildings, and kill people. The ideal rather had something to do with being gentle.

It is perchance because of this that the term is increasingly considered to be an archaism.

Geometry, *n.* [Gk. *geo*, earth, *metros*, measure] A branch of mathematics flowing out of the ancient Greeks' desire to measure the earth. It was adopted by the medieval Scholastics as a means of preparing the mind for the study of theology; their study of geometry often found its culmination when the student crossed the Bridge of Asses. Followers in this tradition held the ancient, Euclidean development of geometry to be God's geometry. They refused to accept as legitimate other axiomatic systems, vigorously attacking Riemannian geometry, which has axioms describing curved rather than flat surfaces.

Gerrymandering, *n.* In modern democracy, the fine art of manipulating certain parts (known as districts) of an ancient artifact from the days before computers, called the Electoral

College. Properly done gerrymandering will increase the weight of some votes and nullify the effect of others, in order to ensure with near certainty that elections will yield the outcome desired by the incumbents.

Golf, *n.* A sport so named because all of the other four letter words were taken.

Goto, *v.* The F-bomb of programming language constructs. It has been observed, "A programmer is someone who, when told to 'Go to Hell,' is offended, not by the 'Hell', but by the 'goto.'" See also: *Pointer.*

Government, *n.* One of several areas the subject of an insightful philosophical commentary entitled the Tao Te Ching. Composed in China by Lao Tzu in 500 BC, it paints a picture of government that is like acting; only bad acting draws attention to itself, and the best acting causes the observer to forget the fact that he is watching actors. This book is the origin of the words, "Running a big government is like frying a small fish," popular among Republicans. (There are also statements that Democrats would like, but Democrats do not believe in reading books) A small fish is fried without being cut up or cleaned; that is to say, with a minimum of interference. Hence Republicans like to quote the words as a reason to avoid spending money on social programs and other uses that they dislike (spending ample money on programs that they do like, such as military expenditures and subsidies for environmentally destructive business, is, of course, exempt). Although this may not have been the original intent of the words, there is another significant way in which running a big government is like frying a small fish: it is very inefficient.

GIMP, *n.* Greatly Irritating Mystification Program. Proof that a graphical user interface can be every bit as arcane, uncontrollable, and frustrating as *any* text interface.

Gnosticism, *n.* A major Early Christian era heresy. At its root, Gnosticism contained the idea that the spiritual is good, but the physical is evil.

Perhaps the most deadly aspect of Gnostic error was the denial of Christ's manhood. Knowing that Christ was fully divine, and believing that the physical was evil, Gnostics deduced that Christ could not possibly have been a carnal creature like you and me with real, tangible flesh. They even went so far as to declare Christ's body to be an illusion.

Only slightly less problematic was the denial of the fact that God himself created the material word as good. The Psalms thank him for his gifts of bread, oil, and wine; the depths of the sea and the stars of the sky declare the glory of their Creator; Paul quoted the Psalms as saying, "The earth is the Lord's, and everything in it," encouraging believers to eat whatever was sold in the meat market without raising any question on ground of conscience. So far from believing that the material world was created by God as good, some Gnostics went so far as to state that Satan created it when God wasn't looking; they embraced a patently false dichotomy between the physical and the spiritual. The word 'scathing' is perhaps an understatement in describing some of Paul's reactions:

> Now, the Spirit expressly says that in later times, some will renounce the faith, paying attention to deceitful spirits and the teachings of demons, through the hypocrisy of liars whose consciences are seared with a hot iron. They forbid marriage and demand abstinence from foods, which God created to be received by those who believe and know the truth. For everything created by God is good, and nothing is to be rejected, for it is sanctified by God's word and by prayer.

I Tim 4:1-5, NRSV

Gnostic heresy has, fortunately, been eradicated, and the church's abstimeniousness ever since serves as an inspiration to us all.

Gospel According to Thomas, *n.* An ancient writing representing the full, second century development of Gnostic thought, now subject to consideration for inclusion as a canonical writing.

Grace, *n.* The one blessing that people strive to earn more than any other.

Grammarian, *n.* A person who studies the most common patterns of word order as they appear in language. After they are catalogued, the descriptions become ossified and canonical prescriptions; anyone who dare write in a manner contrary to the grammarian's edict because such writing seems more natural or fluid is corrected, and, if impenitent, blacklisted.

> Heckler (to Churchill): Mr. Churchill, you end far too many of your sentences with prepositions.
>
> Churchill: I take all sorts of criticism in this business, but that is the sort of criticism up with which I shall not put!

Great Commission, *n.* A commandment of Christ taken to be central by believers who live and die in fulfillment of his words in Matthew 23:15:

> All authority in Heaven and on Earth has been given unto me. Go therefore, and make converts of all nations, baptizing them in the name of the Father, and of the Son, and of the Holy Spirit. And I will be with you always, to the end of the age.

-The Truly Not Inspired Version

Guard, *n.* (1) An armed brute entrusted with the responsibility of keeping people from escaping imprisonment. (2) A complete set of rules around the insufficient set established in Scripture, given limited support in I Cor. 4:6 and Deut. 4:2. Due to the fallenness of human nature, the fact that we do not live in a perfect world, and the powerlessness of the Holy Spirit, the naive and simplistic ideas generated by God's inferior wisdom are not enough; a guard around the law is necessary in order to prevent transgression against the moral laws. While few have managed to duplicate the exacting precision and completeness of the Pharisees' Guard around the Law, it must be said that there are many who are carrying on their worthy tradition.

> Being instated as an archangel, Satan made himself multifariously objectionable and was finally expelled from Heaven. Halfway in his descent he paused, bent his head in thought a moment and at last went back. "There is one favor I should like to ask," said he.
>
> "Name it."
>
> "Man, I understand, is about to be created. He will need laws."
>
> "What, wretch! you his appointed adversary, charged from the dawn of eternity with hatred of his soul--you ask for the right to make his laws?"
>
> "Pardon; what I have to ask is that he be permitted to make them himself."
>
> It was so ordered.
>
> -Ambrose Bierce, *The Devil's Dictionary*

Happiness, *n*. A state which is created by some wherever they go, and by others whenever they go.

Haemorrhoid, *n*. See *Boil*.

Hatred, *n*. The coward's response to the unknown.

Heretic, *n*. One who, while appreciating the overall truth of the Christian message, is wiser than God and recognizes certain errors in orthodox theology. These errors usually occur at some point where God misinterpreted the nature of love.

Jesus summarized the Law in the commandments to love God and neighbor, and the teaching of the Apostles retained this; we are bestowed grace, the outpouring of God's love, a love which is to transform and fill us. Love for neighbor is so important that, oftentimes, the way to love God is through obeying the commandment "Love your neighbor"; in the Sermon on the Mount, Jesus said, "If you are in the temple offering a sacrifice and remember that your brother has something against you, go, leave your sacrifice on the altar, and be reconciled with your brother." Heretics have generally retained an understanding of the central importance of love for a neighbor, and offer a better way to do so.

It seems, as time passes, that the zeitgeist is a continual source of heresy. Of course, it is not the only one, and most major heresies have been able to claim at least a few adherents for most of time, but the spirit of the time seems to aid the most people in recognizing that the Bible is an old book, and bring Christian thought and application of the Law of Love into accordance with the most recent discoveries.

In the nineteenth century and early twentieth, the law of the jungle was understood, and lovingly applied to human affairs. In the wild, only the strong shall survive. It seems harsh, but is far more merciful than mercy. It is sad for a weakling to be killed, it is conceded, but necessary; if the weaklings survive to pass on their inferior genes, it is whole future generations which are doomed to be weakened, and experience a slow and painful death. Mercy is penny wise and pound foolish. Even when people aren't killed, there is often something to be done to make sure that they do not infest future generations with their inferior seed; hence the involuntary sterilization of the mentally retarded. By eliminating mercy, and allowing all those who would pass genetic disease and infirmity to be preyed upon, it is possible to ensure that future generations are strong, healthy, and happy; this was believed to be the best way to apply love.

Now, even among people who believe casuistry to be the best way to adhere to moral imperatives, that misinterpretation is passe. It is recognized that people are equal and have a right to live, and that different is not necessarily evil. From this, it is deduced that being different automatically precludes the possibility of evil, and, if people are equal, then all tendencies are equally good, equally consistent with a state of health and fullness of life, equally resultant from the state of a person in good physical, mental, and spiritual health. Paul was mistaken when he, having declared redemption for sinners and a life of freedom and joy to those who submit their sinfulness to God's grace, declared homosexual practice to be inconsonant with holy living. Past generations were wrong to burn homosexuals at the stake; we avoid their error by recognizing that homosexual practice was created by God as good, as evidenced by the words from Genesis which Jesus quoted to answer the question about divorce: "He created them male and female."

Highway, *n.* A route of transit more dangerous than airplanes at the height of terrorist crises, calmly travelled by people who would never set foot inside a jet.

Holocaust, *n.* One of the most revolting moments in history, when Hitler murdered six million Jews. In the midst of this horrible tragedy, we have learned lessons which will never be forgotten. We have learned to do a better job of ignoring genocide, as we have done for half a dozen other events which exceed the number of Jews Hitler destroyed, or at least use a better name, like 'ethnic cleansing'.

Holy War, *n.* A war which is especially unholy.

Homo Sapiens, *n.* [Lat. man the knowing] The scientific name for man.

Common men seem to have no difficulty deciding, "Is that entity over there a man or a beast?"

To scientists and philosophers, though, it is not such a straightforward question. They are in pursuit of the one action which sets apart man from the beasts.

Some value technology, measuring the progress of a civilization's culture, morality, and character by the machines it produces. Thus, the distinguishing feature between man and beast is the ability to use tools. But even some birds use twigs in order to get food.

Now, language seems to be the prime locus of attention. The distinguishing feature is the use of words, that is symbols, to communicate. But dolphins do that. So it's really the ability to put words or symbols together in new grammatical combinations -- or at least was, until it was discovered that a chimpanzee can do that, too.

This present lexicographer is unaware of any beasts which consider it necessary to spend time arguing about what it is that sets them apart from other species, let alone understand doing and being, accident and substance, well enough to confuse them.

Hospitality, *n.* One of many virtues lost in modern life.

Hubris, *n.* The attitude of one who refuses to see things my way. A popular word among relativists.

Hymn, *n.* The sacred song of the Reformations, where the teachings of the priesthood of the believer and the holiness of everyday living are applied to the realm of music.

The music of the Catholic Church was and is beautiful, ancient, powerful, stately, and majestic; nobody had accused Rome of disgracing God by poor taste in music. The reason that the Reformers used different music was as an application of another part of their theology.

The Reformers held to the priesthood of the believer; they believed that a farmer as well as a missionary can and should draw close to God. To this end they translated the Scriptures into the common tongue, to reach people where they were. They also held belief in the sanctity of everyday living; prayer and study of the Scriptures are the sacred privilege and duty of the believer, but the believer also gives glory to God by eating and drinking, working and playing. Pulling these thoughts together, they used popular tunes as the medium to carry teaching in verse. Although the songs lacked any complexity -- the musical equivalent of flat soda -- and cannot honestly be described as embodying good musical taste, even those songs were taken and transformed. The Roman Church had slowly fallen into the error of making Christianity something far off, boring and unintelligible sermons and odd songs with prayers and incantations in a dead language, elite and aloof from the way that common people live; the Reformers wished to cleanse the Church of this error. The Holy Scriptures, formerly available only in the Latin of the Vulgate Versio, were now rendered in the vulgar tongue, and people began to sing of Christ's love to the tune of popular drinking songs -- all to reach out, and place the Gospel message before people, meeting them where they are.

This beautiful thought has not been forgotten; cherished hymns sung by the Reformers have been passed down from generation to generation, and used to keep Christian youth from becoming entangled in the Devil's music.

IBM, *n*. I've Been Mugged. A mismanaged behemoth which has designed and engineered the line of computers which has been the industry standard in personal computing for decades. Everybody has a skeleton hidden in a closet somewhere.

Icon, *n*. An idol in competition with the true Christian's devotion to the Bible.

Idealistic, *adj*. 1: [philosophical usage] Holding the belief that there exist minds, sensations, and thought processes within those minds, but not an external material world to which sensations correspond. 2: [common usage] A patronizing and condescending term used in reference to a person who holds unswervingly to the only moral standards there are, implicitly declaring those beliefs to be as disconnected with reality as those of a person who is idealistic in the first sense.

What the word says is that such uncompromising faithfulness to the call of conscience is not to be praised (at least not beyond half-insults of "He means well." and "His heart is in the right place.") but, rather, gently patted on the head and politely dismissed. What the term *means* is that the speaker, whose own compromised conduct has been brought to light by that of person referred to, and suddenly looks very shabby -- indeed, all the worse for its whitewash coat of noble-sounding words about how "We do not live in a perfect world." and so on and so forth -- is not only justified in compromise and lowering of standards, but actually doing a better job than someone who does not compromise: the speaker is more truly on the mark, and the idealistic one has the most praiseworthy intentions but misses the goal in an excess of misguided zeal. To top it all off, the word is not recognized as a pungent insult such as 'asinine' or 'idiotic', but pleasantly accepted as a simple statement of the way things are.

See also: *Admirable*, *Values*.

Idiot box, *n*. An ingenious device which stimulates the senses and bypasses sense.

Ignore, *v*. To imitate American Christianity's treatment of the Biblical teachings on wealth.

Illustration, *n*. In childrens' Bibles, an iconoclast's depiction of important Bible characters and stories. The difference between an illustration and an icon is that the illustration is not venerated, and with good reason. Illustrations recall characteristic moments from important stories by representing the characters involved. By so doing, they teach many important truths, the first and foremost of which is that Jesus was white.

Incoherent, *adj*. Lacking internal consistency; muddled and confused. An account is said to be incoherent if no sane person could hope to make sense of it. Incoherence dates back to the result of the attempt to build the Tower of Babel, as recorded in the book of Genesis:

And they said to one another, "Come, let us make bricks, and burn them thoroughly." And they had brick for stone, and bitumen for mortar. Then they said, "Come, let us build ourselves a city, and a tower with its top in the heavens, and let us make a name for ourselves; otherwise we shall be scattered abroad upon the face of the whole earth."

The Lord came down to see the city and the tower, which mortals had built. And the Lord said, "Look, they are one people, and they have all one language; and this is only the beginning of what they will do; nothing that they propose will be impossible for them. Come, let us go down, and confuse their language there, so that they will not understand one another's speech."

And there was Kuhn.

-The New Revised Nonstandard Version

Incompetent, *adj*. Very well paid.

Those who can -- do.

Those who can't do -- teach.

Those who can't teach -- administrate.

Those who can't administrate -- do it anyway.

-Author(s) unknown.

Incongruity, *n*. The basis for modern life.

Indescribable, *adj*. About to be given a very poor description.

Indicator, *n*. A kind of marker which, when measured or examined by a competent observer, will reveal more macroscopic information about a system. In ecology, certain species are very sensitive to environmental conditions; thus their population serves as a good indicator of the health of an ecosystem -- such as red algae.

In the early days of aerial warfare, engineers understood and appreciated the delicate balance between armor and agility. They devised airplanes as best they could, and then observed the results of combat in order to make a more effective machine.

In order to accomplish this, they had a life sized picture of an airplane. Every time an airplane came back from combat, they would place a dot on the picture corresponding to each bullet hole. By so doing, they hoped to discern exactly where the most damage was sustained, and thus intelligently place armor as effectively as possible.

It was eventually noted that there were no dots over the fuel tank.

Inefficient, *adj*. Resembling the methods and practices currently in use.

Infallible, *adj*. Not subject to doctrinal error. It is believed by Catholics that the Pope is infallible, which is absurd; no single man is infallible except for me.

Infest, *v*. For something foreign to enter an organism and cause it to rot. For example, meditation, a practice of Eastern religions, has been carried to the west in the degenerate form of New Age. The abhorrent activity is beginning to infest nearly all facets of Christianity, and is rumored to penetrate even the purity of the Early Christians.

Inflammable, *adj*. Flammable.

Inhuman, *adj*. Acting without a shred of human decency; demonic; resembling the soldiers (and civilians) we are destroying in the current war.

Inn, *n*. In former times, a precursor to the modern hotel.

> Once upon a time, a wayfarer came upon an in bearing a sign, "Inn of Saint George and Ye Dragon." He knocked upon the door, and the matron came out.
>
> "Pray have mercy on a poor and weary traveller beset by bandits. I've got no silver, but I can sing or tell a tale."
>
> "I care not about the woes of a filthy ragamuffin. Begone." With these words, she threw a rotten apple at him, slamming shut the door.
>
> He began to walk away, paused in thought, and at last returned, once again lifting the heavy knocker.
>
> "What?"
>
> "May I please speak with Saint George?"
>
> -Reader's Digest

Innumerate, *adj*. Lacking in basic mathematical (number) skills, just as 'illiterate' refers to someone lacking basic reading (letter) skills. The latter is recognized as a severe handicap and fought accordingly; the former is accepted because thinking hurts. There are three types of people in America: those who remember rudimentary mathematical skills, and those who have forgotten them.

In Parentis Loco, *n*. See *Loco*.

Inquisition, *n.* A systematic attempt to remove heretics by executing heresy.

Insomniac, *n.* One most prepared to appreciate the most prominent quality of the *Lord of the Rings*.

Institutionalized Food Service, *n.* A special case in which the law of gravity is reversed: what goes down must come up.

Intel, *n.* The company that put the 'backwards' into 'backwards compatibility.'

International Law, *n.* Law that is violated in multiple countries instead of just one.

Intimidation, *n.* In American diplomatic theory, the basis for cultural sensitivity and achievement of understanding.

> Westley (to gatekeeper): "Where is the gate key?"
>
> Gatekeeper: "There is no gate key."
>
> Westley (to Fezzik): "Fezzik, tear his arms off."
>
> Gatekeeper: "Oh, you mean this gate key."
>
> -The Princess Bride

Intuition, *n.* A means of thought thought to be proven useless by logical people because it has not been rigorously proven according to logical methods.

Journalist, *n.* One engaged in the pursuit and obscurement of important facts.

Jury, *n.* A group of peers selected to render judgment, on a basis of inability to identify with any of the involved parties.

Kinder and Gentler, *adj*. Crueler and harsher.

It is obviously evil to beat or molest a child. What is less obvious, an ever so sweetly disguides sadism, consists in a manner of parenting that is always pleasant and rosy.

The basis for parenting is love, and a child is not a punching bag to scream at or hit after a bad day. It is wrong to strike a child in anger, and a spanking can only be right if it is more painful to the parent than the child.

That being true, a parent who is loving and wise must chastise and administer painful discipline as a tool of correction. He who fails to do this raises a child who is spoiled.

This child will not understand consequence on anything more than an immediate physical level; he will not burn himself by placing his hand on a hot stove only because his parents lack the power to make the action painless. In all other areas -- conduct towards other people, thievery, promiscuity -- he will do whatever seems most attractive at the moment. The belief that some things are worth a wait, or the idea of action bearing consequence, especially a delayed consequence that does not come by physical mechanism, is a foreign concept. And so, when the child could be entering into life, he is instead trapped in the abyss of self.

This present lexicographer wonders how long it will be until those under the 'kinder and gentler' mindset will be told to go to Hell -- not by man, but by God.

Klu Klux Klan, *n*. See *Klueless Klux Klan*.

Koinonia, *n*. The life in community and fellowship shared by believers. The Early Christians lived in a world where people identified and separated themselves by race, social class, and gender; the Church astonished the world by showing Jews and Greeks, masters and slaves, males and females, who not only did not exhibit the same tensions, but were all one, together, equal, in Christ Jesus. Today in our nation Christians gather at 10:00 AM, the most segregated hour of the week.

Kneejerk Liberalism, *n.* Liberalism's strand of a thread which runs through nearly all parts of society. Kneejerk liberalism is largely responsible for the "Stop nuclear power in order to save the environment." and the "Shut up in the name of open-mindedness and free speech!" movement, among others. Kneejerk conservatism, not terribly different, encompasses most Rush Limbaugh listeners.

Of course, kneejerk movements are not limited to the political sphere. Also to be mentioned is a kneejerk following of science, which believes science to have displaced God and the appropriateness of religious faith, kneejerk openmindedness, which attacks Christian thought and any other intellectual edifice which is built on a foundation unlike its own foundation of relativism (which turns out to span most of human thought over most of time), and kneejerk spirituality, also known as New Age.

> **Idiot**, *n.* A member of a large and powerful tribe whose influence in human affairs has always been dominant and controlling. The idiot's activity is not confined to any special field of thought or action, but "pervades and regulates the whole."...
>
> -Ambrose Bierce, *The Devil's Dictionary*

Knock, *v.* (1) To strike a light blow which does no damage against a door or other massive object, in the hope that it will open. (2) [colloq.] To strike a light blow which does no damage against a ridiculous law or other massive object, in the hope of opening and illuminating information which is not plainly seen. In this sense, the word is almost always used pejoratively.

Know-Nothing, *n.* A member of an extinct political party formerly of great influence in American public life.

Labor-Saving Device, *n.* Any one of a number of inventions which is common among people who are busy, and scarce among people who have leisure.

Landfill, *n.* A storage device used in the preservation of biodegradable materials.

Lazer, *n.* Light Amplified by Stimulated Electromagnetic Radiation.

Lehi, *n.* A battle between Samson and the Philistines, when a multitude was slain by the jawbone of an ass. Its pivotal importance is recognized, so that there have been many historical re-enactments worldwide.

Lent, *n.* A special time of year set aside for solemn prayer and fasting. It is customary to use this time to contemplate Paul's words about special days and seasons.

Liberal, *adj.* and *n.* A scholar desiring to correct the tendency of conservatism and tradition to slowly and imperceptibly tarnish and distort that which they attempt to preserve. The liberal scholar studies the ancient origins in their original form, and then attempts to remedy the situation by offering fresh, new heresies.

Lifeboat Ethics, *n.* One of many fine-sounding and respected excuses for a lack of ethics.

Lifestyle, *n.* That mode of preaching which espouses an alternative set of doctrines.

Like, *tic.* In Valspeak, a continual reminder of "Look, I'm Klueless, Etc."

Light Bulb, *n.* An invention which permits electricity to travel through a tiny filament. The filament puts up tremendous resistance to this, using the energy to generate approximately 5% light and 95% heat. Herein lies the Western precept of illumination.

Liquor Law, *n.* A form of regulation found in the places most plagued by alcoholism, teaching children to regard drinking as an adult activity (the ability to drink friends under the table being the true test of maturity), and, in some states, prohibiting parents from training children in the temperate and controlled use of liquors.

Literate, *adj.* Innumerate.

Lottery, *n.* See *Poverty Tax, Gullibility Tax.*

Love, *n.* A technical detail of secondary importance to the basis of morality, the Ten Commandments.

Lutheran, *n.* Pertaining to a denomination in the tradition of Martin Luther, a man who avoided the error of the church in Laodicaea, accused in Revelation of being neither hot nor cold, by being both hot and cold. Luther made many adamant statements, among them an insistance of, "Do not ever name a denomination after me."

Luxury, *n.* A rare pleasure availiable only to a privileged few, such as being able to walk. It is important to distinguish luxuries from necessities, such as driving a car.

MacCuisinart, *n.* The ultimate word processor, doing to words what food processors do to foods.

Machiavellian Politics, *n.* Politics.

Macintosh, *n.* (1) An apple distinguished for its sweetness, colorful lustre, and lack of meat. (2) A computer, with a name perhaps chosen for the acronym "Mouse Activated Computer", sporting software designed around the central parameter of requiring the user to do nothing sufficiently complicated to confuse a mouse. A striking example of the essential identity of agriculture and computer science.

Majority Text, *n.* The most accurate Greek New Testament text. While it was the accepted text for over a millenium, there have been since discovered some other texts. These inferior texts reflect considerable modification and transmission errors, and sometimes have entire verses missing; they have hindered the work of translators for over a century.

Marxism, *n.* A system of thought named after Karl Marx, who said, "Religion is the opium of the people,", and, coincidentally, lived before the invention of television.

Mascot, *n.* An animal chosen to symbolize or represent a team or entity, thought to embody those qualities that it values most. A political cartoon depicted the Democratic party as an ass, a representation which was meant as an insult, but was happily accepted. The Republican party, feeling jealousy at not having a mascot, selected as its mascot the elephant, the one remaining member of an otherwise extinct family. The other members, such as mammoths and mastodons, were big, slow, and died because they could not adapt to their environment.

Maze, *n.* A puzzle and test of human intelligence. It consists of an intricate system of walls, the objective being to move from the entrance to the exit. It is commonly represented on paper, as if viewed from above. Most people can solve such a puzzle quite well. If actually inside the puzzle, such as the hedge mazes sometimes found at wealthy mansions, human performance is poorer, but still comparable to that of the average rat.

Memorization, *n.* A filing system used by those who are too lazy to look details up.

Memory, *n.* A faculty that, in our culture,

Micro$oft, *n.* The company which has produced a flight simulator which is the industry standard for testing the robustness of PC emulators. Its products are phenomenal to the extent that they are, in advertisement, something which people swear by, and, in practice, something which people swear at.

Minimalism, *n.* An aesthetic which avoids cluttered design by keeping detail and beauty to a minimum.

MIPS, *n.* Meaningless Indicator of Processor Speed. The expression was originally thought to mean Millions of Instructions Per Second, until Sega produced a video game system with a substantially higher MIPS rating than a Cray supercomputer. There are other numerical ratings thought to be of equal accuracy, but the discreet lexicographer does not name them.

Misnomer, *v.* An inaccurate expression, inappropriately used to refer to something which it does not describe. Ex: 'Catholic', 'Orthodox', 'Protestant'.

Mock, *v.* To render the highest form of compliment due the bulk of modern philosophy.

Moderation, *n.* One of the four cardinal virtues of classical antiquity. In modern times, it is held in light esteem; most people wish to replace it with either the virtue of Abstention, or the virtue of Excess.

Modern Art, *n.* A French expression meaning 'Art Nouveau.'

Money, *n.* A blessing which is appreciated and generously given in proportion to the amount possessed -- inverse proportion.

Monopoly, *n.* A classic bored game, commonly pronounced 'Monotony'.

Monroe Doctrine, *n.* A bold stance from early American history. Even in its infancy, the young democracy was asserting itself with the strength and leadership which would eventually lead to its role as the world policeman.

Monty Python, *n.* An anti-intellectual form of comedy which is extremely popular among intellectuals.

Moon, *n.* A celestial body which, after long training and observation, people learn not to see during the day.

Moral, *n.* That for which the unenlightened take mores, and which the ever so different enlightened take for mores.

Moral Majority, *n.* Neither.

Morning, *n.* A time of day as joyous as its homonym.

Motor Oil, *n.* The preferred cooking oil of institutional food services everywhere.

Motorcycle Lane, *n.* A shortcut to the wages of sin.

MS-DOS, *n.* A major medical breakthrough of the 19th century, providing modern medicine with what many doctors still consider to be the most effective known treatment for hypotension.

MtG, *n.* Magic, the Gathering. A commercial gaming product (legal, de$pite a level of addictivene$$ by which it mu$t be $aid that $moking i$ a comparatively ea$y habit to break) of $ufficiently fiendi$h cleverne$$ to make T$R executive$ cur$e in awe.

MTV, *n.* As stated by the Russian author Solzeneitsyn, "the liquid manure of Western culture."

Multiculturalism, *n.* A deity offered much worship and veneration. Of all the gods of the current pantheon -- Mammon, Technology, Postmodernism, Psychology -- perhaps the one whom one is most persecuted for failing to bow down and worship.

Multilingual, *adj*. Proficient in the use of multiple languages. In certain parts of Africa, it is not unusual for a person to speak five or six languages; worldwide, the average is somewhat lower, but most places still appreciate the importance of being able to use a language other than the native tongue. A person who can speak three languages is trilingual; a person who can speak two languages is bilingual; a person who can speak but one language is American.

Mushroom, *n.* and *v.* (1) A fungus which is kept in the dark and fed an ample supply of manure. (2) To grow and expand beyond all proportion. A striking example of how much administration is able to requisition to its own purposes.

Narrow-Minded Bigot, *n.* Someone who is white, is male, is Christian, appreciates the heritage of Western Europe, and/or holds and speaks beliefs which cannot properly be expressed in a slightly late implementation of George

Orwell's Newspeak.

Nation, *n.* A country or people. In Old Testament times, the nation favored by God was Israel; now that Christ has come, the nation is America. Isaiah's Messianic prophesies clearly predict America as Christ's chosen nation:

> Of the increase of the Federal Government there shall be no end.
>
> -The Unauthorized Version

Natural Selection, *n.* The proposed mechanism, according to Darwin's account, of evolutionary change. It states that organisms which are better suited to their environment survive and pass on their traits, whereas more poorly suited organisms do not. Its capital defect is its total failure to provide any explanation for the continued survival of Incomestibilis spammus.

NBC, *n.* National Broadcasting Company. One of several similar television companies, all of which vastly exceed most of public broadcasting stations in airing programming which is stimulating and edifying. Appreciation for how often such services should be used is believed to have inspired a military acronym referring to nuclear, biological, and chemical weapons.

Necessity, *n.* The mother of invention. Profit is the father.

New World Order, *n.* See *New World Disorder.*

New Year's Day, *n.* In the Christian calendar based on the year of our Lord, a holiday occurring six days after Christmas.

NIV, *n.* Now Indispensible Version. This translation is one of the best modern English translations of the Holy Scriptures. It has achieved a wonderful balance between word for word and thought for thought, and rightly become immensely popular and widely used. All Scripture is God-breathed, and the scholars creating this translation started from scratch to give what has turned out to be, in many cases, excellent renditions of the original meanings. The donors and administrators over the scholars were sufficiently wise to avoid the temptation of telling the scholars to set aside professional judgment in favor of what they thought a Bible should and shouldn't be. See also: *Bowlderize*.

Non-Alcoholic Beer, *n*. Beer that has been watered down until it can legally be sold as a non-alcoholic beverage.

Non Sequitur, *n*. Therefore, Al is a pud.

Normal, *adj*. What you think other people are like.

NOW, *n*. National Organization of Women. An organization which fought tooth and nail to ensure that women as well as men are permitted to serve in the military, but has not lifted a finger to see that women are subject to selective service.

NPC, *adj*. Not Politically Correct. Correct.

NRA, *n*. National Rifle Association. That group which is working vigorously to defend our constitutional "right to keep and bear firearms", while recognizing the datedness of the words, "as part of a well-regulated militia."

NRSV, *n*. Not Really Sure Version. The culmination of many reworked and revised translations tracing back to the King James, this translation holds several singular virtues. With the knowledge that it might be used for liturgical and other reading, the translators tried to produce a rendition with smooth assonance. Yet they knew that there is something even more important than natural sounding English. Unlike practically all other translations, this translation admirably avoids, at all costs, introducing gender bias which was not present in the original languages. For example, words in Revelation 2:23, where Christ is speaking to the angel of the church in Thyatira, is generally rendered something like "I am he [sic] who searches hearts and minds."; it is instead rendered "I am the one who searches hearts and minds." This avoids the possibility that Christ might be offended to hear a more sexist rendering of her words.

NSA, *n.* National Security Agency. The government agency responsible for ensuring that nationally used encryption algorithms are insecure.

Nuclear Power, *n.* A means of using nuclear rather than chemical reactions to generate electricity, which is orders of magnitude more efficient. A nuclear plant's waste is contained in a bushel sized encasement rather than emitted ton upon ton upon ton by billowing smokestacks. It is, pound for pound, worse than any other known residue, but minute in amount, well-contained and easy to deal with; a coal burning plant incidentally generates higher levels of radioactive waste, which are not considered worth paying attention to in the shadow of the damage done through carbon dioxide, soot, and so on. The one weakness of nuclear power is expense; it costs more per kilowatt-hour than any other widely used method of generating electricity. Nuclear power is staunchly supported by most conservatives and adamantly opposed by most environmentalists.

Nude, *adj*. Ahead of fashion trends.

Number, *n.* The most common mathematical entity used to lend buoyancy to an insubstantial argument, and strike awe and gullibility into the hearts of people who lack a rudimentary understanding of mathematics. Research has shown that

73.2% of all statistics represent poorly gathered or inaccurate original data, 87.9% of all statistics are substantially manipulated and distorted in the form in which they are finally presented, and 99.5% of the remaining statistics are made up on the spot.

NutWare, *n.* A secure networked operating system which usually requires the proper password before granting supervisor privileges.

Oath, *n.* A solemn and officially recognized declaration of one's lack of trustworthiness.

Obfuscation, *n.* A quality which is generally added to bolster Christianity's natural weaknesses.

Obvious, *adj.* Considered to be unworthy of attention; unnoted.

"It is the first duty of intellectuals to state the obvious."

-George Orwell

Official Endorsement, *n.* A highly effective means of destroying a religion when intense persecution has failed.

Oleoresin Capiscum, *n.* See *Non-Alcoholic Firebreather.*

One Size Fits All, *adj.* See *One Size Fits None.*

Open-Minded, *adj.* Ready to vigorously attack anyone who seriously challenges an orthodoxy of academic freedom in all areas.

Optimize, *v.* To produce alterations to a section of code which will decrease runtime and resource consumption without interfering with its utility.

Audience member (to speaker): "Is there a Unix

FORTRAN optimizer?"

Speaker: "Yes. 'rm *.f'"

Opulence, *n*. The quintessence of the lifestyle of many spiritually impoverished people who have sealed their ears to Biblical teachings about wealth. The most prominent and definitive feature of American Christianity.

Organ Donor Card, *n*. The flipside of a driver's license.

Ossification, *n*. The universal result of administrative attempts to preserve an organization's strength and vitality.

Painkiller, *n*. A drug which kills the ability to deal with pain, taken as a symbol of American culture.

Pangloss, *n*. In Voltaire's novel Candide, a teacher expounding the most pessimistic and cynical of known doctrines.

Parliament, *n*. [Fr. *parler*, to talk] A form of legislature which attempts to resolve hot issues by the exchange of hot air. American government has branches with names other than 'parliament', apparently for the same reason that some states have names such as 'The People's Republic of China'.

Pascal, *n*. A handholding pseudolanguage whose students have insisted on dragging into the real world to abuse as a language.

Pax, *n*. [Lat.] Peace. This word is occasionally used to refer to specific cases of peace, such as the *Pax Romana* and the *Pax Americana*. It also has meaning within a religious context, in reference to the kiss of peace.

The language used in the New Testament in reference to the believers is not one of separated people who happen to share beliefs, maintaining a curtain of isolation and afraid to come near each other; it is instead a family. The picture painted is one of an intimate community; language that referred to the believers as brothers and sisters was used in Scripture, and repeated in the words and lifestyles of the Early Christians.

In this sense, it is not at all surprising that the Apostles wrote their letters to the churches, and, along the practical instructions usually included towards the end, included personal greetings, by name, and commanded a warm embrace. "Greet one another with a holy kiss." "Greet one another with a holy kiss." "Greet one another with a holy kiss." "Greet all the saints in Christ Jesus." "Greet all the brothers and sisters with a holy kiss." "Greet those who love us in the faith." "Greet all your leaders and all God's people." "Greet one another with a kiss of love." "Greet the friends by name."

The kiss of peace began to be formalized as a part of the liturgy. The Scriptures certainly do not forbid a greeting within such a context, but the kiss of peace is never mentioned in connection with any ceremony. As centuries passed, it somehow seemed not to occur too much outside of the ceremony. After a few centuries, in order to avoid impropriety, the practice was modified so that only men were permitted to greet men, an only women were permitted to greet women. But that still involved touching, and so there appeared a most interesting invention: an object called the Pax.

The Pax was a small pendant or amulet, worn for the sake of services. It was held out to be kissed.

And so, the troublesome command to "Greet one another with a holy kiss." was thus dealt with, in an ingenious manner which obviated any occasion for people to touch each other.

It is fortunate that this manner of dealing with the wisdom laid out in Scripture has not occured anywhere else.

PC, *adj*. Politically Correct. Political Correctness is avoidance of certain words judged to embody closedmindedness and prejudice (and ostracism of anyone who does). For example, 'm-nk-nd' is deemed an inappropriate word to use to refer to all members of Homo sapiens, because the word 'm-n' (which originally did not specify gender) has come to sometimes mean a perbeing who is specifically male. Thus, the only reason anyone would say 'm-nk-nd' is out of spite towards every womyn. Political Correctness is a wonderful thing; many people have it to be an excellent substitute for actually removing prejudice.

PC-USA, *n*. Politically Correct, USA. A church in which there is neither heterosexuality nor homosexuality, monotheism nor polytheism, orthodoxy nor heresy.

Peace through Strength, *n*. Establishing peace, according to your own terms, by ensuring that your nation has superior military powers to those of its neighbors. With the advent of nuclear weaponry, peace through strength has taken a new step forward and now also bears the title of mutually assured destruction.

Paradoxically, this is actually not as absurd as it initially sounds. It works remarkably well due to an essential unity of spirit among the nations. Peace is desirable. That is the almost unequivocal consensus. Military strength is the best way to achieve this -- again, the nations' consensus.

Thus each nation attempts to establish a military that is a safe margin greater than the forces of its neighbors. This helps prepare for the resolution of any misunderstandings that might arise. In addition, the resulting friendly competition does wonders for the economy, especially on the poorer end.

Pejorative, *adj*. Embodying a low opinion; said of words. 'Pigheaded', as contrasted to 'resolute'. The word 'dog', when used in reference to human beings, is an extremely pejorative term, embodying more contempt than most obscenities. It is in this sense that the word was used by Moses in reference to male shrine prostitutes, and by Paul, in reference to men who took it upon themselves to supplement the ordering force of the Holy Spirit with additional rules.

Penitentiary, *n*. An academy whose expenses are paid by state scholarships, improving select pupils' skills in the clandestine arts and reinforcing their impenitence.

Pentacostalism, *n*. A movement which remembers and believes in the gifts of the Spirit as described in the New Testament, while demonstrating a remarkable forgetfulness for New Testament instructions as to how those gifts are to be used.

People's Democratic Republic of Korea, *n*. One for four.

Perception, *n*. That by which we see (and hear, feel, smell, taste) a combination of the world around us and what we expect to see. Most people, of course, believe that we only observe the former, and this is very useful for practical jokes.

> ...it is necessary to pay close attention to the most minute detail.
>
> -Inspector Clouseau

Perfect World, *n*. A hypothetical situation vastly removed from the reality we live in. For the past 1700 years, it has been fashionable to assume that the inhabitants of a perfect world are the only (hypothetical) people to whom the Sermon on the Mount is addressed.

Pesticide, *n.* A chemical agent used to increase the population of pests by making them immune to poison and by destroying their natural predators.

Peter Principle, *n.* A piercing insight into the function of American business.

The Peter Principle states, in essence, that individuals in an organization will rise to their level of incompetence. That is to say, a person who demonstrates competence in one field will be "promoted". A promotion consists of an increase in pay, and hours of time expected to complete responsibilities, combined with a shifting of responsibilities to another field requiring a different skill and talent. This philosophy of promotion holds that the various functions within an organization -- which may be likened to parts of a body -- are to be ranked and ordered, so that when one part excels at being itself, it is considered to be evidently good at being the next part up. A bicep muscle which proves its strength and stamina is surgically removed from the upper arm and reattached to the end of the wrist and expected to grasp and do fine manipulation; a nose which keenly picks up faint odors is transplanted to the eye socket and expected to see. Thus, the more competent an individual demonstrates himself in handling one set of responsibilities, the more likely he will be to be reassigned to another field where he is incompetent. See also: *Incompetent*, *Promotion*.

Pharisee, *n.* A member of an extinct religious sect frequently mentioned in Scripture. Most churches have recognized the importance of presenting the whole of the Gospel in modern and accessible terms rather than those obscure and ancient. They thus mention Pharisees and what Christ said to them far less frequently than they hold seminars on how to use technicalities and loopholes to minimize the financial inconvenience caused by income tax.

Philosopher, *n.* [Gk. *philos*, love, *sophia*, wisdom] A man who loves wisdom and truth. The philosopher pursues these matters with all of his mind, striving to be united to truth, to know her most intimately and completely, and, like a jealous husband, does his best to prevent others from doing the same.

Phonetically, *adj*. A word which isn't spelled that way.

Photobiodegradable Plastic, *n.* Photobiodisintegrable plastic.

This substance consists of an ordinary plastic film mixed with a small fraction of biodegradable material such that, given time and sunlight, it will disintegrate into innumerable microscopic particles. The particles are then engulfed by microbes, causing them to die in a way that a nonbiodegradable film could not come close to.

The substance is made to be environmentally friendly.

Pinnacle, *n.* The highest point. To literal usage, "the pinnacle of the mountain" etc., has been added figurative usage, "the pinnacle of his career" etc., to refer to the highest point which cannot get any higher.

It is illuminating, in this case, to look at synonyms and antonyms. The idea of a highest, crowning top point is expressed by a number of synonyms, from apex to zenith. It is then perhaps all the more notable that antonyms, expressing the concept of a sunken abyss from which it is not possible to get lower, simply do not exist.

This fact is, in the view of this present lexicographer, not a coincidence. Words appear in number, variety, and subtlety to suit the needs of the people using them; hence the Eskimos have approximately twenty different words referring to different kinds of snow, and we, whose lives are not nearly so directly affected, have only made a couple ('powder', 'slush'). Words are used to express concepts that reflect people's thought, and there is perhaps very good reason that we do not have any word to use for an (for lack of a better term) anti-pinnacle.

On television, the Simpsons appeared as the anti-pinnacle of their genre, a low point at which things simply cannot get any worse. Then came Beavis and Butthead. Barney the Purple Dinosaur appeared as the most annoying and distasteful anti-pinnacle of children's fads. Then came the Mighty Morphin' Power Rangers.

Dare we assume that it is impossible to get any worse than the view of causality embodied in NBC's Dateline?

Pipe, *n.* A feature of UNIX, enabling the output of one process to be the input of another. *Purgamentum init, purgamentum exit.*

Pocohontas, *n.* G-rated pornography.

Poison, *n.* An elemental or chemical agent which, when introduced to an organism by contact, inhalation, or ingestion, induces reactions which are harmful or lethal. Poison has historically been associated with assassins, an extremely dishonorable lot which refuses to rely exclusively on firearms to commit murder as civilized men do. There are many known poisons. Most of the heavier elements, such as lead, mercury, selenium, administratium, and so on, are poisonous. The biological world has produced hosts of organic poisons; industry observed this, and realized that it might be able to gain substantial profits by providing assassins with a superior variety of products. This prospect was successful beyond all expectation, and now provides millions of jobs, forming a stable and respected pillar of the economy. Realizing that openly advertising products for use in assassinations could be a potential legal liability, poisons are effectively concealed behind a front that markets them as fertilizers, fuels, cleaning agents...

Political Correctness, *n.* See *Newspeak.*

Pop Psychology, *n.* Nonsense.

Pope, *n.* (1) The bishop upon the See of Rome. In the Apostolic Succession, the Pope carries the torch handed down from Peter, the rock upon whom Christ built his Church. He acts as the capstone of the College of Bishops and his infallibility is established in Saint Paul's Epistle to the Galatians, ii.11, and affirmed by Tradition. (2) As used in several early English translations of the Bible, designed to avoid the Catholic Church's monstrous tendency to hide or distort Scripture to suit its purposes, an alternative rendering of a word frequently translated 'Antichrist'.

Popular Taste, *n.* See *Popular Distaste*.

Postmodernism, *n.* The cadaver left over after philosophy has committed suicide.

Pride, *n.* A substance whose foul and bitter taste we do not fully realize until we have swallowed it.

Priest, *n.* A man of special sanctity, imbued with the authority to serve as an intermediary between man and God.

The priestly office is very clearly outlined in the Old Testament, the priests uniquely holding the authority to offer sacrifices, to enter into holy places, and to consume sacred foods. The highest priest, once each year, was permitted through the blood of a sacrificial victim to enter into the most sacred of places, the Holy of Holies.

The New Testament speaks also of priesthood. The Old Testament sacrifices were a shadow anticipating the things to come, for Christianity is to know priestly office in its fullest. Christ is the ultimate priest, having a priesthood after the order of Melchizedek, both priest and victim, who offered the one perfect sacrifice for all time. By the most precious blood he entered into the Holy of Holies, and has not merely permitted but called all believers in him to enter with him to the Holy of Holies also. He calls all believers, offering to them the most sacred of sacred foods. And, in the greatest mystery of priestly mysteries, orthodox Christianity sets aside some believers set aside as especially holy to hold the authority to act as priests, performing duties and rites not permitted to the laity.

Priority, *n.* An objective which is taken to be of prime importance. A person or nation's priorities can be very rcvcaling.

> We have grasped the mystery of the atom and rejected the Sermon on the Mount.
>
> -General Omar Bradley

Professor, *n.* In the modern academic world, a researcher whose performance is evaluated primarily on a basis of the amount of unnecessary articles he publishes.

Progress, *n.* Noted advancement in one area combined with unnoted retrogression in many others.

Promotion, *n.* A financial incentive offered by corporate mismanagement to an employee who has demonstrated competence in one set of responsibilities to assume another, in the hope of finding a field of incompetence.

Prophet, *n.* An unauthorized preacher whose message is offensive to the guardians of orthodoxy. See also: *Martyr*

Prostitute, *n.* A wretched woman created to help us appreciate the security of our own spiritual position. See also: *Pharisee*

Protest, *n.* A check on abuse of power emphatically protected in the Bill of Rights, granting freedom of speech and the right to peaceably assemble. The people who established these most pre-eminent and vital of amendments to the United States Constitution realized that corrupt regimes shield themselves from correction and reform by making speaking out against the government a punishable offense. Thus one of the Founding Fathers declared the importance of freedom of speech in the words, "I disagree with what you say, sir, but I will fight to the death for your right to say it." Today the torch is honorably carried by the Democratic Party and the American Civil Liberties Union, who vigorously defend the rights to freedom of speech and peaceable assembly, provided that they are not exercised in a manner that involves protesting an abortion clinic.

Protestant, *adj.* and *n.* A believer who is not Catholic or Orthodox. Unlike the other two, Protestants do not have a continuous line from the beginning. Rather, they broke off (sometimes voluntarily, sometimes involuntarily) from the Catholic Church, believing that the adherence to Tradition was inappropriately obscuring Scriptural teaching, such as James's doctrine of salvation by faith and faith alone. They held to the doctrine of Sola Scriptura, meaning that they would not take Tradition as a basis for doctrine, but instead only use the Scriptures which supported their views. Today, still holding strongly to Sola Scriptura and other important traditions, they have seminaries (attendance to which is requisite to clerical positions) which teach the faith from extensive creeds and confessions, designed to remove the confusing task of directly interpreting the Scriptures.

Puppetry, *n.* A form of art appreciated in most of the world. It is shunned in America, and relegated to children. Only a child would have the imagination to succeed in believing that a couple of pieces of cloth are characters woven into a story. Mature adults do not watch puppet shows, but rather respect and demand movies with exquisite lighting, sets, acting, and special effects; oftentimes, they are so well done that they are difficult to distinguish from real life. This, also, explains the complexity, sophistication, subtlety, and depth to be found in plots.

Puppy, *n.* A warm and soft animal handled and enjoyed by people who are afraid to touch each other.

For an infant, touch is every bit as important a need as food and protection from the elements, if not moreso. A baby deprived of touch will, quite literally, wither and die.

If a puppy is taken into some place with a lot of people, there will be a shower of people wanting to pet it. Part of this is due to how cute it is, and it must be said that there is nothing which feels quite like a puppy's fur. At the same time, there is another factor also at play.

Handling a puppy, purring cat, guinea pig, or some other agreeable furball, is one of a few situations where social mores are actually willing to interpret an innocent touch as an innocent touch. There are allowances made for exceptional circumstances, such as moments of great sorrow and the handling of young children, but even these are not entirely steady; it is actually illegal in some states for a kindergarden teacher to give a student a hug, so fervent is the legal zeal to avoid sexual misconduct.

Thus, we have embraced the age old style of solving problems, so greatly concerned with respecting people's space and, as touch rightly plays a vital role in marital union, avoiding what could possibly be taken to be unwanted sexual advances, that human contact is deemed expendable and unnecessary, a frying pan which we must jump out of at all costs. See also: *Pax*, *Purity*, *Victorianism*, *Wealth.*

Purity, *n.* A virtue to be found in that which is free of any taint of evil. Purity should pervade not only actions but thought. Its relentless pursuit is perhaps best illustrated by the following story, which has come to us from Buddhist folklore:

> There were two monks, finally returning to their monastery at the end of a long trip. They were passing through a wooded region, forest with scattered paths and villages.
>
> Walking along the road, they came to a large clearing. Cutting through the clearing was a river, with stepping stones across. There had been a great storm the night before, and the river was flowing swiftly, sweeping over its banks and the stepping stones.
>
> There was a young woman standing on the near side of the river, holding a bundle of firewood, clearly wanting to cross the river, but terrified to do so, not trusting her light frame against the currents.
>
> The older of the two monks, who was a tall and very stout fellow, set down his walking stick, and walked over. He picked the girl up.
>
> Slosh. Slosh. Slosh. He still had to try to maintain his balance, but he got to the other side and set her down.

Slosh. Slosh. Slosh. He picked up his staff, and then continued walking with the other monk.

After about an hour, the younger monk spoke.

"I know that you are older and wiser than I, and perhaps I should not be speaking. But there is something that I wonder."

"Speak, my child."

"To be a monk means to take a vow of celibacy. Perhaps I do not understand, but was it right for you to hold a young girl like that?"

The older monk walked a few steps, and then drew a deep breath. Finally, he spoke.

"Oh, my child. Are you still carrying her?"

Quebec Separatism, *n.* A political movement distinguished from the Rhinoceros Party chiefly by its inability to recognize when it is being hilariously funny.

Qwerty, *adj.* and *n.* A keyboard layout created in the nineteenth century, with many the most frequently used letters under the weakest fingers. The qwerty layout was used when primitive typewriters would easily jam, in order to slow down typists and keep them from typing too quickly, cutting typing speeds by over 40%. Now, even the crudest keyboards are capable of handling any typing speed without jamming, but the rule is still qwerty, kept for over a century by secretaries and other typists who can't be slowed down by taking the time to learn another keyboard design. See also: *MS-DOS*

Rabbi, *n.* See *Reverend.*

Racism, *n*. Egotism taking the form of a delusion that one's own race is less depraved and idiotic than the criminal tendencies and gross stupidity exhibited by another.

Random Number, *n*. In computer science, the output of a deterministic algorithm carefully designed to produce output according to a specific distribution, deemed far too important to leave to chance.

Rank, *adj*. and *n*. (1) A numerical rating of a person's skills -- "Better than him, not as good as her" -- taken as a measure of worth. (2) Possessing a putrescent stench.

Rationalism, *n*. The first step in the flight from reason.

Rationalist, *n*. One who holds an irrational faith in the human mind.

Recursion, *n*. An extremely powerful concept (or non-concept, depending on perspective), whereby the set of functions and procedures potentially invoked by a function or procedure includes itself. See also: *Algorithm*, *Function*, *GNU*, *PINE*, *Procedure*, *Recursion*.

Red, *adj*. and *n*. The color of roses, sunsets, and many ideologies.

Red Russian, *n*. One of the followers of the regime that made for Stalin, and supported an implementation of a somewhat altered version of communism (an economic system which has functioned at its best at monasteries, nunneries, and other religious communities to which a vow of poverty is requisite) which tried to keep religion under tight control. The implementators of the Russian and Soviet implementations of communism were masters in the use of symbol; an even more notable addition to the communist implementation of Utopian ideals was captured in the color of the flag.

Redundancy, *n.* (1) Repeated statements of the same thing. (2) Saying the same thing over and over again. (3) Language or wording which is repetitive. (4) Something which is cherished by many orators. (5) Phrasing which duplicates its meaning many times over. (6) ...

Regurgitate, *v.* (1) To expel from the mouth material which has entered the stomach and been found unsuitable to retain. (2) To expel from the mouth material which has not entered the brain.

Relationship, *n.* A kind of box that people expect to take treasures out of without placing anything of value into, first.

Relativism, *n.* The philosophical system of those who have finally come to realize that all truth is entirely a matter of perspective.

Religion Within the Bounds of Reason, *n.* The thinking man's way of remaking God in the image of his mind.

Renaissance, *n.* A time of intellectual rebirth, when many things -- from philosophy to art -- were rethought and infused with new energy.

The movement in art is perhaps most striking. On one level, there was an awesome mastery of technical detail, from the use of perspective to da Vinci's subtle use of blue to create distance in the Madonna of the Rocks.

The skill which they used succeeded in creating more convincing illusions than ever before. The term "Renaissance Masters" is quite justly applied to these artists, but the most profound rethinking of Renaissance art was not on a technical level.

Jesus was a Middle Eastern peasant, with calloused hands

and skin darkened by years' beating in the sun. The Renaissance Masters invariably showed him to be a soft and fair skinned Caucasian, who most definitely did not look Jewish; the Jews (in the rare instance that they were painted) were a symbol of conniving, greed, and rejection of everything that is good, and so they knew far better than to paint Jesus as a dark-skinned Jew.

Jesus was a carpenter by profession, and he completely violated people's expectations of a rabbi. He chose disciples, but not from the scribes and lawyers, the educated and literate. Instead, he chose a very motley crew of manual laborers -- fishermen and whatnot, even one terrorist thrown in for good measure. The Renaissance Masters, in painting the disciples, knew that Jesus would only choose men attired in dignity; his disciples are invariably painted as Greek philosophers.

His birth was announced to shepherds, in one of the great images of the last being first. A shepherd was crude, dirty, smelly, and uncouth; he could outswear a Roman soldier, and his testimony was not legally valid in a court of law. They might be described as the ancient equivalent of used car salesmen, except for the fact that the modern used car salesman does not have quite that bad of a reputation. From the Renaissance onwards, the image of the shepherd has been used as an image of the pastoral, to symbolize everything that is calm, serene, peaceful, and idyllic; the angels are painted as joining this beautiful scene to sing of the newborn Messiah because of how perfect it is.

An angel, as described in Scripture, is invariably majestic, awesome, and terrifying. Their first words are almost always "Fear not!", to calm the great fear that comes in response to such a magnificent creature of power and light; when they appeared at the Resurrection, their presence was sufficient to make soldiers faint from terror, and John, after seeing all things in Revelation, fell down at the angel's feet to worship him. The Renaissance Masters had the skill of brush to capture something of this majesty, and painted angels as voluptuous women whose clothing is always falling off.

The Renaissance Masters would be pleased to see the wonders of television news reporting.

Repair, *n.* A polite word meaning 'kludge.'

> Duct tape is like the force. It has a light side and a dark side, and it holds the universe together.
>
> -Carl Zwanzig

Repeat, *n.* To render greater persuasive force to a weak argument.

In advertisement, the most ridiculous claims -- AT&T is preferable to MCI because it is only slightly more expensive, if you drink our beer, you will be surrounded by models in bikinis, our dish soap is superior because it contains real lemon juice, our car is accompanied by a woman in a miniskirt, whenever there's fun there's always Coca-Cola, women flock to a man who wears our underwear before having a chance to guess what brand it is, smoking cigarettes will make you strong and healthy like this cowboy, if you buy our camera you will have a consort almost wearing a very interesting outfit, you will have an orgasm while eating our ice cream, and so on -- are rendered persuasive by the force of repitition. The force is so powerful that, costs being passed to the customer, consumers purchase these more expensive products rather than generic brands, and do so with frequency that makes multimillion dollar advertising expenditures pay for themselves several times over. At least the mindless repitition of risible nonsense provides a relaxing diversion from watching political speeches.

Responsibility, *n.* The long-lost twin of freedom.

Revere, *v.* To hold in a high degree of respect and affection. For causing people to feel as if they are thinking, one is revered, and for causing people to think, detested.

Revolutionary, *n.* A person attempting to establish a Utopian society by wading through blood. If this attempt to remove corruption and oppression succeeds, the insurrection becomes a revolution. The revolution is like a point on a wheel, slowly rising out of the muck and mire as it revolves around its axis.

Rock, *n.* (1) In the natural world, a stone. (2) In the musical world, a form of entertainment enjoyed by those who wish to become stone deaf.

Rose, *n.* A flower of singular beauty, holding a unique place in romance and some celebrations. The rose has a stem covered with sharp thorns, and, with full knowledge of the thorns, people still appreciate its breathtaking beauty enough that it is said that a rose is God's autograph. It is exceptional in more ways than one.

RSV, *n.* Revised Standard Version. In the first edition, a dangerous mistranslation heretically discordant with the authority of popular opinion.

From the reactions it received one might be tempted to think that they gave an accurate rendition of a comment Paul made in Phillippians. Paul listed many reasons he had to be confident on his own, without need of grace: born into the tribe of Benjamin, circumcised on the eighth day, perfect in maintaining ceremonial law, flawless in Pharisaic legalism, ad nauseum. A couple of verses later, he commented on their real value: "Furthermore, I consider everything a loss next to the surpassing greatness of knowing Christ Jesus my Lord, for whose sake I have lost all things. I consider them all ----, that I may gain Christ." He was perhaps contemplating the rebuke of the Divine through the prophet Malachi:

> And now, O priests, this commandment is for you. If you will not listen, if you will not lay it to heart to give glory to my name, says Yahweh Sabaoth, then I will send the curse on you; truly, I have already cursed them, because you do not lay it to heart. I will wither your offspring, and spread ---- on your faces, the ---- of your solemn feasts, and drive you out of my presence.

or perhaps the words of the prophet Isaiah, who compared righteous acts to a used tampon.

A like reaction might be be generated by rendering the crowd's words about Jesus "Crucify him!" in words the same hate took over a millenium later: "He is a faggot. Burn him at the stake!" Perhaps there were footnotes explaining that the word *stauros* (in its various forms) was not merely a pejorative term, but an obscenity.

Or perhaps a dynamic equivalent of the Song of Songs, rendering the sexual metaphors and double entendres in fresh English. Perhaps they might have rendered "His banner over me is love." in a less literal manner, more understandable to the modern reader, so that Sunday School teachers would be less sorely tempted to set it to an annoying tune and teach it as a song to young children. Perhaps they departed from the Victorian classic describing that which is described between the legs and belly and likened to a rounded goblet flowing with wine: the woman's navel.

But they did none of these, choosing an error far worse.

In Hebrew, the word meaning 'young woman' was spoken with the implicit understanding that the young woman is a virgin. The prophet Isaiah recorded the word of Yahweh, "Behold, the young woman shall be pregnant and shall give birth to a son, and call his name Emmanuel..." RSV in its first edition not only rendered the word as 'young woman' (with a footnote saying 'or virgin'), but placed in footnotes (rather than the main text) various verses which are not found in the most ancient and reliable manuscripts, preceding the editing work of Erasmus in creating the Textus Receptus.

As a result, the RSV became a banned book. It was held up and waved around as the latest Communist-Marxist-trying to subvert the doctrine of the virgin birth-heretical-Catholic-infiltration. *En masse*.

This prompted the creation of RSV Second Edition, a work less offensive to such staunch Christians.

Rule, *n*. The shuffled off husk of morality.

Russian Orthodox Church, *n*. A church in which, the higher you go up in the heirarchy, the less faith there is -- right up to the top, where requisite to membership in the Ministry of Religion is a profession of atheism.

Sacred Cow, *n*. A ridiculous superstition which benighted fools dare not give five minutes' serious re-examination, protected by a careful line of Things You Do Not Question, as contrasted to the incontestable wisdom of our own feminism, lesbigay movement, multiculturalism, relativism, humanism, progress, materialism...

Safe Sex, *n*. In modern times, a second rate (not to mention dangerous) substitute for the original safe sex.

Safety, *n.* Avoiding or minimizing the risk of human injury. For example, during Operation Desert Storm, safety was such a high concern in operational procedures that U.S. forces achieved a kill ratio of better than 100:1 of Iraqi civilians to U.S. soldiers.

Salad Bar, *n.* A conglomeration of circles, lines, cylinders, rectangles, fractals, and so on, serving a function which, in centuries past, was served by the formal study of geometry.

Secure, *adj.* Replete with undiscovered security holes.

Seminary, *n.* An academy devoted to the study of the highest sacred truths, and to the integration of faith, learning, and life.

Time is fleeting. Resources are short. In the best of all possible worlds, we might be able to make any compromises, but we do not live in the best of all possible worlds. Constantine taught us that.

In an experiment conducted by some psychologists, a class of divinity students, one by one, was sent off (belatedly, due to bad planning) and told, as a final exam, to hurry over and give an expository sermon on the meaning of Luke 10:30-37.

The experimenters, in order to test them, had placed certain distractions in the way of the students -- even a person who was made to appear injured and in need of medical assistance. Practically none of them shirked their true duty, but went on to give the sermon without wasting any of their professors' time.

Truly, if the head of the house embodies such

unimpeachable character, we need not hold any doubts about the spiritual condition of those living within the house.

Sensitivity, *n.* One of the prime concerns of administrators and directors, who desire to use their power and authority in such a manner as to benefit those under their authority. In order to effect this proper use of power, it is important to be attuned to the needs and desires of those people; it is an administrator's business not to be aloof. This quality is best demonstrated in an immortal story from hacker folklore:

> In the beginning was the Board of Directors. And the Board of Directors formed the Administration. And the Administration formed a Committee. And the Committee formed the Plan.
>
> The Board of Directors believed that the Plan was good, but wished to be sensitive to the Hackers. They did not wish to use the Plan, except that the Hackers Approved.
>
> So they sent Memos explaining the Plan, and Low Level Administration summoned the Hackers to set aside their Work and attend Meetings, to find what the Hackers thought of the Plan.
>
> "You, the Hackers, are our life's blood. Our strength as a Corporation depends on you; you are the source of our Success, and we hold the highest Regard and Appreciation for your Wisdom. Now, you have had time to read and meditate upon the Plan. What do you think? Is the Plan a good or a bad Idea?"
>
> "It's a crock of ----, and *it stinks!*"
>
> Then Middle Level Administration summoned Low

Level Administration to set aside their Work of wasting the Time of the Hackers, and attend Meetings, to explain what the Hackers think of the Plan.

"You have spoken with the Hackers. The Hackers are very Intelligent, and have many good Ideas. What do they say of the Plan?"

"It is Manure, and the Stench thereof is Great."

Then Upper Level Administration summoned Middle Level Administration, to set aside their Work, and attend Meetings, to explain what the Hackers think of the Plan.

"You have spoken with those who have condensed the wise and good Ideas of the Hackers. What do the Hackers say of the Plan?"

"It is Fertilizer, and it Smells of great Power."

Then the Board of Directors summoned Upper Level Administration, to set aside their Work, and attend Meetings, to explain what the Hackers think of the Plan.

"You know the Wisdom and Understanding of the Hackers, and what they believe of the Plan. Our Time is scarce, so we are certain that you can explain their Reactions briefly. What do the Hackers say of the Plan?"

"It promoteth Growth, and the Vigor thereof is exceedingly Great."

Whereby the Board of Directors was greatly Pleased,

to learn that the Hackers appreciated the Value, Efficiency, and Wisdom of the Plan.

And the Plan was Approved, and made Action.

Sermon, *n.* A speech used in a church service to instruct believers in sound doctrine and holy lifestyle. This ecclesiastical function is very important, enough so that it is occasionally misunderstood to be the focus of a worship service.

Sometimes, to make a sermon easier to remember, the preacher will center it around a certain number of points. Hence there will be a sermon on the four spiritual laws, seven points of effective prayer, the three 'P's of resisting temptation, and so on. There is some controversy over how many points a good sermon should contain; the best have at least one.

Sesame Street, *n.* Education within the bounds of amusement.

Settler, *n.* Someone who goes to inhabit land already inhabited by other people who are of a different race and whose lives are thus considered worthless.

Sex, *n.* One of the God-given blessings of which different cultures are most universally intolerant.

The most obvious example of this is found in the most ridiculously idiotic monument of Victorian culture. Victorian thought held that, because the marriage bed is private, it is to be an object of shame. While claiming to be Christian, Victorian thought flaunted a blatant disregard for the Song of Songs, an extended commentary on the words in Genesis, "Male and female he created them." and "Two shall become one," and utterly ignored Paul's words, commanding that the husband and wife should yield to each other's conjugal rights. The Victorian mind found sex to be, at best, an unfortunate but necessary evil in order to produce children. Hence, in a letter to a newlywed bride, a minister commanded that she give occasionally, give sparingly, and give grudgingly; what they were to have as sex precluded the possibility of seeing each other's bodies, and, if the husband began to fondle or kiss anywhere not strictly necessary in order to produce children, the wife was suddenly to excuse herself.

Current American culture, by contrast, considers sex to be a faceless, underclothed, and underweight model holding a product in an advertisement, or, taken further, still little more than a cheap thrill, to toy with when other forms of amusement become boring. Sex is not a cherished bond, a union of body, mind, and soul that encompasses conversation and silent walks as well as foreplay and intercourse, best described by the word 'know'; this present lexicographer is reminded of monks who used pieces of the oldest known Septuagint manuscript to start fires.

People who have cohabited and quickly introduced intercourse to romance wonder why sex after marriage seems a contradiction in terms; along with adulterers, they are befuddled at why it is so difficult to keep a marriage together. Even the people who recognize certain limits are inclined to ask, "How far can I go?" rather than, "How much do I want to have left?"

The harm stemming from a culture using pornographic magazines and casual sex is not that its people experience too much sex, but that they experience too little.

Herein lies a very illuminating glimpse of American culture.

Sexual Harassment, *n.* (1) In a court of law, an unwanted sexual advance. (2) Under educational administration and corporate mismanagement, any statement, supportive hand-on-shoulder, door opening, gesture, facial expression, et cetera, which could possibly be misinterpreted as having sexual overtones. (3) In the future, any handshake, polite greeting, eye contact, presence in the same room, et cetera, which cannot positively be proven not to have any sexual overtimes.

Sexual Misconduct, *n.* A charge which must be taken seriously if the accused is conservative, but should be carefully examined if the accused is liberal.

Sharp's, *n.* Flat's.

Shock, *n.* The state of any sane person upon seeing how far our world has fallen. Something which people learn to ignore to retain their sanity.

> We have lost the invaluable faculty of being shocked.
>
> -C.S. Lewis

Shoot, *n.* The most common mispronunciation of '----'. Used by people who desire the force of an expletive, while retaining a sense of self-righteousness at refrain from language which refined people do not use.

Sight, *n.* A faculty of perception which permits us to forget that we have four others.

> Your ambush would have been more successful if you bathed more frequently.
>
> -Worf

Sin, *n.* An expert remodeler whose services are in great demand for the maintenance and preservation of institutions and traditions. His competitor has some very satisfied customers, but is generally considered far more difficult to trust.

Sinister, *adj*. Shadowy; mysterious; dark; abysmal; in short, evil. Etymologically, the word signifies left-handedness.

People who are left-handed tend to be intuitive, original, and creative; in short, different. And so, historically, most of them have either been taught to be right-handed, or mercifully burned at the stake.

It is a rare society which does not declare at least some of what is harmless to be evil, and some of what is evil to be harmless.

Sit Com, *n*. Situational Comedy. A form of televised annoyance in which the placement of flat and predictable characters in stupid and embarassing situations is confused with comedy.

Skin-deep, *adj*. About as far as most people look.

Sleep, *v*. To "celebrate with appropriate ceremony" the content of a political speech.

> Opposing speaker (to Churchill): Winston Churchill, *must* you sleep while I am speaking?
>
> Churchill: No, it is purely voluntary.

Small Talk, *n*. The fine art of having nothing to say and saying it anyway.

Smoking, *n*. A legalized form of suicide.

Snob, *n*. A man made arrogant by money, looking down on normal people as if they were urchins, and possessing more wealth than I do.

Sociology, *n.* The enlightened liberal's way of reducing everyone to a collection of stereotypes.

Sola Scriptura, *n.* [Lat. *sola*, only, *Scriptura*, Scripture] A momentous doctrine of the Reformation, holding that only the Scriptures are to be used as a basis for teaching.

Scripture has held an important role in church history; it is God-breathed and profitable for teaching and rebuking, in its entirety. If a belief contradicts the unambiguous teaching of the Scriptures, it is an error; only a heretic would hold so low of a regard for these sacred writings as to hold even one out and say of it, "It is a letter of straw. Burn it."

If the Scriptures are to be magnified beyond being seen as a final resolution as to which doctrines are and are not acceptable, and declared to be the only acceptable source of teaching, then it is important to see what they are and what they do and do not say.

The Scriptures are an anthology of a wide variety of sacred writings. A definition is not the place to quote a thousand pages of truth, but there are a few points which are notable here. The Scriptures do say that God himself speaks through the lips of prophets, and the Creation declares the glory of its Creator. They do not, at any point, give a listing of which works are to be considered canonical.

Sophia, *n.* [Gk.] Wisdom, which, along with knowledge (*gnosis*), was considered by Gnosticism to be the route to salvation. The Gnostic understanding of wisdom -- of attaining the spiritual by shunning the physical, of balancing and then moving beyond good and evil, of a Christ whose prime purpose was to offer knowledge rather than to offer grace, and so on -- was harshly attacked by the Apostles and Early Fathers. Recent thought has found that some of these ideas are perhaps better than they were thought to be, and bits and pieces have slowly been brought into Christian thought. The work is far from complete, of course, but there have been many steps to follow in the path of the Gnostics and wholeheartedly embrace a system of ideas worth its weight in gold.

Sorceror's Bargain, *n.* A classic pact with the Devil, who offers, "I will give you power if you give me your soul." But there is a problem (aside from the obvious difficulty of the power having no value near that of the soul): if you make the deal, it isn't really you that has the power. Once the deal is made, it is a lose-lose situation.

In the contemporary Western world, the sorceror's bargain is frequently made with two very attractive looking twin demons, named Mammon and Technology.

Both of them woo people with the sweetest promises, never speaking of any price to be paid. And both of them somewhere, somehow, find the most creative ways to extract payment (and deliver more of an illusion than a reality of what they promised). . It is notable that, in the Sermon on the Mount, Christ's warning was not "No man can own two slaves," but "No man can serve two masters."

> Calvin: I had a dream last night in which machines had taken over the world and made us do their bidding.
>
> Hobbes: That must have been scary.
>
> Calvin: It sure wa--holy, would you look at the time? My TV show is on!
>
> -Calvin and Hobbes

Sorcery, *n.* The study and practice of spells, evocations, incantations, gestures, and so on, in an attempt to divine the future and manipulate unseen forces to produce supernatural effects. Out of sorcery the practice of science has sprung. Science then began to spurn even the most remote trace of magic, and has now progressed to the point of being indistinguishable from it.

Sore Loser, *n.* A very poor sport whom I will only play if he is the only one I can beat.

Sound Bite, *n.* In contemporary life, the basis for public miscourse and the illusion of thought.

Source Criticism, *n.* The proper scholarly response to texts that are clearly the result of incompetent editors attempting to interweave entirely distinct sources, as evidenced by the fact that the texts are not written according to the standards that a modern scholar would use.

Sovereignty Association, *n.* All of the benefits of being a part of Canada combined with none of the costs.

SPA, *n.* Software Publisher's Association. An association of software publishers which seeks to stamp out the problem of software piracy by the use of intimidation, and coercion when people do not surrender, to extract ransoms from anyone unfortunate enough to cross their waters.

Speed Limit, *n.* A maximum speed, assigned by laws which prohibit cars from moving more than ten miles per hour less than the average road speed in the country, or faster than ten times the average road speed in the city.

Spherical, *adj.* Appropriate for consideration in physics calculations.

Splinter, *n.* A small fragment of wood, which often manages to work its way into the hand. A splinter in the thumb has never been popular, but nothing matches the swiftness of a person trying to deal with the true sting caused by a splinter in the eye.

Once upon a time, a man came to a psychiatrist.

"Doc, wherever I go, whatever I look at, all I can see or think of is sex, sex, sex. Can you tell me what's going on?"

"I think so, but I'd like to run a few ink blot tests first. I'm going to hold up some sheets of paper with colored spots, and I want you to tell me what you see.

Walking over to a shelf, he pulled a binder, and, opening it, began to hold up sheets of paper.

"What's this a picture of?"

"Sex."

"Ok, what's this a picture of?"

"Sex."

"What about this one?"

"Sex."

"Can you explain how?"

"Yes. Right here, you can see that the..."

Thirty, forty, fifty ink blots. Always the same response -- "Sex.", "Sex.", "Sex."

Setting down the binder, the psychiatrist opened his desk drawer, and pulled out two sheets of paper from there -- one

8 1/2 x 11" blue lined sheet of notebook paper, and one blank 8 1/2 x 11" sheet of typing paper.

"All right. Those images are somewhat old, and perhaps all look more or less the same. I want you to clear your mind of all thought, and then I'm going to hold up two more sheets of paper, different from any of the ones before. Could you please tell me what you see?"

The psychiatrist, with one swift motion, lifted both sheets off the desk, holding them up in the air for the patient to see.

"They are both graphic sexual images, like all the rest."

Even after profesional training, the psychiatrist was somewhat taken aback; he wasn't expecting that reaction. Caught off guard, he said, "Well, um, I see. You do seem to have a one track mind."

"Hey, Doc! *You're* the one who's drawing all of the dirty pictures."

Standard, *n.* Any one of a number of officially endorsed options, enabling the individual a wide variety of options.

Statistician, *n.* A skilled advertiser with at least a BS in mathematics.

> There are three types of lies: lies, damn lies, and statistics.
>
> -Mark Twain

Statue of Liberty, *n.* An immense and awe inspiring statue, a powerful symbol of all that is American, beautiful but hollow. The Statue boldly proclaims the magnificent words,

"Give me your tired, your hungry, your poor, your wretched masses yearning to be free," and stands over Ellis Island, the site of immigration offices which, at a time which is seeing a growing gap between rich and poor and (quite possibly) seen more large scale genocides than the rest of history, enforces strict maximum quotas on the number of immigrants who are permitted to enter the country.

Stupidity, *n.* See *Drive-Thru Liquor Store*.

Subliminal Message, *n.* William H. Everston's new theory, helping/enabling commercial organizations' ugly new traps. Richard Y. Inglenook stopped this hideous, rastifarian outrage. What next? In no trick observed, children have acted or served, potentially, as truly rational. Inglenook observes that idiots seldom muse. It should be obvious right now.

Subtlety, *n.* [obs.] An attribute of good writing, where the meaning is not immediately obvious, requiring thought to understand.

Suggestion Box, *n.* An unusual garden set up by administrators. They till the soil, spreading an ample amount of fertilizer, and then allow others to come and plant whatever seed best expresses their sentiments. The administrators then come, weeding out those plants which are troublesome, and nourishing and exhibiting those which are compatible with the administrators' goals and plans.

Suntan, *n.* A precursor to wrinkles and melanomas, deemed to be highly attractive by a culture whose models of beauty are almost never born with dark skin.

Supercomputer, *n.* A computer which is a few years behind the needs of industry and research, combining the latest in hardware with the most primitive of software.

> You can tell how far we have to go, when FORTRAN is the language of supercomputers.
>
> -Steve Feiner

Symbol, *n.* A forgotten art which once represented most of Christian thought.

Systematic Theology, *n.* The mark of the Enlightenment on Christianity, where God is expected to bow down and worship the human mind. A part of wisdom frequently mistaken for the whole.

> **Ritualism**, *n.* A Dutch Garden of God where He may walk in rectilinear freedom, keeping off the grass.

With all due respect, Ambrose Bierce is mistaken in implication. I humbly submit that it is inaccurate to make such a statement of all ritualistic traditions, and ludicrous to imply that ritualism (or, for that matter, systematic theology) has a monopoly on such things.

Tactician, *n.* A man skilled in the methods of persuasion most devoid of tact.

Talk, *v.* To exercise the strongest muscle in the body.

Taoism, *n.* A tradition in Chinese thought dating back to approximately 2500 BC. The tradition began as a profound philosophical system originated by Lao Tzu. From that point, it continually devolved until it finally became a generic pagan religion, complete with gods, priests, temples, altars, complicated rituals, a calendar of holy days, and everything else necessary to make a complete antithesis of all that made the tradition interesting in the first place. Much like Christianity.

Technicolor Yawn, *n.* The best response to the OJ media circus.

Technology, *n.* (1) Any device invented and used by men [ex: a lever]. (2) A result of and substitute for modern Western civilization, empowering the evil which lies inside the human heart to achieve what it could not possibly achieve otherwise.

Teflon, *n.* One of few plastic resins which is actually more chemically stable (and thus less biodegradable) than polystrene plastic or foam (Styrofoam). The difference between the two is that Styrofoam can be recycled into rice cakes.

Telemarketer, *n.* Someone who believes one of the most annoying and offensive invasions of privacy to make a customer better disposed towards a company.

Such a man would expect a bucket thrown into the ocean to yield cold and pure drinking water. Such a man would expect a thistle to yield figs. Such a man would expect a hornet to create honey.

Such a man would expect a soldier, using violence and intimidation at a superior capacity to destroy, to achieve the manifest presence of love, understanding, and respect for the rights and needs of others which is called justice and peace.

> Like a eunuch trying to take a girl's virginity is someone who attempts to achieve justice through force.
>
> -Jesus Ben Sirach

Telephone, *n.* A very poor substitute for reaching out and touching someone.

In a personal conversation with a friend, the text of what is said is of course important, but there is more. Eye contact, touch, and body language are all carriers of personal presence; of such things, only tone of voice is preserved, and even that is often garbled by line static.

As such, telephone conversations are a distant and miserable rendering of enjoying another person's presence, and it is no great surprise that a majority of them are terse and technical: taking the necessary time to say what needs to get across, but not really taking time to slow down and chat. As reported by the Chicago Tribune, fifty percent of phone calls are one way (person to answering machine), and fifty-two percent of residential phone calls do not last for more than a minute. People exchange brief messages and get tasks done, but maintaining friendships and keeping in touch with family is something which seems to happen. And, if there is any real distance between the involved parties (which is often why a phone call is used as a substitute for a personal visit), it costs money by the minute. Touch, eye contact, body language, and an unhurried and relaxed time are all vitally important, and the telephone takes away all of these. One might be tempted to forget all of this by advertising slogans that suggest touch and show the faces of family warmed by each other's presence, but it is still true.

All in all, a quite perfect picture of how not to cultivate relationships with friends and family.

Television, *n.* A font of wisdom poured out upon those who do not have the time to read the Early Fathers.

Temperance Movement, *n.* A movement of people who reject as inappropriate Christ's model of temperate use of alcohol.

Terrorist, *n.* A terrible soldier capable of striking terror into the heart of the most defensible nation in the world.

> The more advanced a system becomes, the more vulnerable to primitive modes of attack.
>
> -Dr. Who

Theology, *n.* [Gk. *theos*, God, *logos*, Word] A discipline now considered essentially distinct from the direct study of the Word of God.

Thermite, *n.* An industrial strength cleaning agent advisable in the care of hardware made by Zenith Data Systems.

Thoughtful, *adj. Non sequitur.*

Thunderstorm, *n.* A spectacular symphony of nature in which rolling thunder complements streaks of lightning against dark and majestic clouds, droplets pour forth to clean the air and make soft ripples in puddles, staining everything a deep and rich shade, the flowers come open and children dance, and civilization dons galoshes and raincoats, muttering about what a bother it is.

Ticklishness, *n.* Proof that God has a sense of humor.

Tide, *n.* The motion of the waters in the ocean, as influenced by the moon phase. See also: *Caucus*.

Tobacco Industry, *n.* A vital and necessary force in our nation's economy.

> The tobacco industry reports that it provides jobs for 2.3 million Americans -- and this does not include physicians, X-ray technicians, nurses, hospital employees, firefighters, dry cleaners, respiratory specialists, pharmacists, morticians and gravediggers.

-Quoted by Ann Landers

Touch, *n*. A source of information which infants naturally use to learn about objects which sight is used to locate, a vital tool to medical professionals to detect injuries and illnesses that the eye cannot see, but not considered worth learning to develop and use by the mainstream of postmedieval Western civilization.

Tourism, *n*. *Veni, vidi, Visa.*

Traffic Law, *n*. The system of laws governing drivers' conduct on state owned roads, to which members of Congress are exempt. This is in accordance with Article I, Section 9 of the Constitution, which commands, "No title of nobility shall be granted by the United States..." See also: *Congressional Medal of Honor.*

Trickle-Down Economics, *n*. A virtually seamless economic system, keeping all but a trickle of money from reaching the hands of the poor.

TV News, *n*. Television [*tele*, far, vision] News. A device which permits us to see that which is far from the truth.

Unborn, *adj*. Not yet born. Among other admirable groups, the Moral Majority has stood firm and uncompromising in its opposition to abortion as the slaughter of unborn children, in addition to correcting the folly of those who would waste valuable time and resources to protect the environment.

Underaged, *adj*. Lacking sufficient age to do some activity maturely. Commonly, the term is used in reference to a person who is deemed by the government to be too young to properly handle alcohol. This legislative attempt to protect youth from improper use of alcohol has had most interesting results in contrast to places such as England where such responsibility is delegated to parents; underaged alcoholics in America outnumber alcoholics in England.

Undocumented, *adj*. Without a proper description.

Undocumented Feature, *n*. *B*ug.

> Any sufficiently advanced technology is indistinguishable from magic.
>
> Arthur C. Clarke
>
> Any sufficiently undocumented code is indistinguishable from magic.
>
> -Some frustrated systems hacker at 3:00 AM

unix, .n the operating system designed by e e cummings

Unprintable, *adj*. Resembling Holy Scripture.

Up-To-Date, *adj*. Having fallen hook, line, and sinker for the latest fad.

UseNet, *n*. A massive experiment currently in progress, funded in large part by the National Science Foundation. Designed to provide decisive evidence in a hot debate involving many notable biologists, including all researchers supporting Creation Science, it is being eagerly monitored by the scientific community. Its unbelievably complex apparatus involves a million monkeys on a million typewriters, and has not (to date) produced anything even remotely resembling Shakespeare.

Randomness, *n*. An element playing an increasing role in the determination of political, public, and private events in American life.

Belladonna, *n.* In Italian a beautiful lady; in English a deadly poison. A striking example of the essential identity of the two tongues.

Witch, *n.* (1) An ugly and repulsive old woman, in a wicked league with the devil. (2) A beautiful and attractive young woman, in wickedness a league beyond the devil.

Bierce is, again, mistaken; as with ritualism, there are at least a few ladies who are not so described, and it is bombastic to assume that women hold a monopoly on the power to delude and set aside wisdom.

Images play as focal of a role in current American culture as they did in the medieval European culture, but the manner is different. In medieval culture, images were symbols; in a cathedral, stained glass windows and statues spoke a rich language and lore, literature for the illiterate. Upon beholding images, a host of meanings would occur; a detail was all that was necessary for a single picture to tell a story. The image was a trigger to thought. Now, the image is a substitute for thought; charisma has displaced reason.

This is candidly illustrated in the outcome of a recent election, where one candidate fared poorly because, though he was a decorated and courageous veteran, his physical appearance was weak and unimpressive.

Alternately, it may be seen in a political commentator whose opinion and thought is held to be of immense weight by many Americans. It would perhaps be inaccurate to describe his figure as chiselled, but his manner and personality enable people to believe, through a scattering of sound bites and quotes out of context, that he has the monopoly on the truth.

The sound bite itself has become the modern unit of debate; in a land that once paid attention to involved political debates lasting for hours, it is now expected that any argument deemed credible must be developped in seconds. Vivid language is certainly not an evil, but neither is it a substitute for thought.

Due to these trends, it is chaos and charisma which carry the day. Once upon a time, acting and politics were distinct professions. Now... For a leader to be charismatic certainly does not preclude being an effective leader, but neither does it guarantee wisdom. In a sense, though, there is one point separating politics and public concensus from a racetrack.

One of the horses has to win.

, *n.* That for which there exists no adequate word.

Valor, *n.* The attribute, embodying bravery and courage, of a soldier who most truly serves his country, without being deterred or intimidated by any threatening menace which stands in the way of the true cause.

Once upon a time, three generals -- one from the Army, one from the Navy, and one from the Air Force -- were discussing and debating the nature of courage. The debate went through the day and long into the night, and, finally, agreed to visit their respective bases, in order to learn something there.

First, they visited a pier. Driving in a car, the Navy general threw his watch into shallow water, ordering a cadet to retrieve it.

The cadet looked at him in fright, and then, when the general repeated the order, dove into the water, retrieving the watch, at the expense of severe injuries.

The general said, "That is courage."

The Army general paused in thought for a moment, and then said, "That is indeed the beginning of courage, but there is a courage yet greater." And so, they went to an Army base.

At the base, as several tanks were driving by, the general suddenly commanded, "Private, stop that tank."

The man immediately ran in front of the tank, and stoically stood, until the tank came and crushed him to death.

"That is true courage."

The general from the Air Force said, "There is yet one base that we have not visited. There is a sense of courage -- great courage -- which both of your forces have shown, but there is a courage, and a true patriotism, which is greater still."

There was a long time of silence, before one of the other generals finally said, "As you wish," and drove to the Air Force base.

Here, at the beginning of a runway, the Air Force general ordered the car stopped. As a plane came in to land, he barked out, "Airman, stop that plane *now!*"

The young cadet immediately snapped to attention, and gave the general a one-fingered salute.

The general leaned back in his seat. "Gentlemen, that is courage."

Values, *n.* [singular, 'value', generally not used] A term/usage chosen by postmodern philosophers such as Nietzche embodying all of the genius of 1984's Newspeak.

The term designates religious or moral beliefs, but, like a great many words, means far more than it designates. The meaning of the word is that one makes a category mistake in actually regarding such beliefs as corresponding or not corresponding to an external reality; they are rather a strictly internal state, like a person's emotional state. One does not speak of right or wrong values; one rather speaks of a person's values, just as one speaks of a person's tastes and preferences, as an arbitrary and subjective attribute of that individual person. The word places such beliefs within that basic category.

Thus, from the outset, any discussion is biased -- no, worse than biased; a bias presents a difficulty to surmount, while 'values' presents a closed door -- against a meaningful consideration of God, or of the moral structure of the universe. Even the term 'atheism' does not quite contain what this does to the discussion; atheism says, "There is an ultimate reality to which beliefs do or do not correspond; God does not exist; beliefs in God are false." -- and this facet of postmodernism, in its definition of values, can't go far enough to say that a belief does or does not correspond to reality. Words such as 'good', 'evil', 'right', 'wrong' 'heroism', 'adultery', 'honesty', 'theft', and so on aren't even allowed to be wrong in what they describe; they describe not an external moral reality, but only a person's internal state.

It can at least be said that a part of this usage's proper meaning is dropped by some speakers, who perhaps do not think far enough to cringe at hearing the words, "our values." But even then -- this lexicographer cannot recall a single instance of someone referring to values as being right or wrong.

All things considered, a most disagreeable word.

Verse, *n.* An ingenious device, facilitating minute study within strict bounds concerning heterodox misinterpretation of Scripture, and most effective deterrent against quotes out of context. A wonderful set of dependable roadbumps, which the road's paver did not have the foresight to provide. See also: *Footnote*

Victorianism, *n.* The death knell to sexual purity in Western culture.

Victorianism held sexual purity to be extremely important. All well and good, but it did not stop there. Victorianism believed sexual purity to be best approached via a Pharisaic guard around the Law. And, like every other guard around the Law, it did a tremendous amount of damage to numerous other things before destroying the very object it was meant to preserve.

Touch and community are vital elements of human health. This is witnessed in Scriptures that tell of John reclining in Jesus's bosom and in the hands quickly extended to pets, one of the few situations where our society will allow an innocent touch to be an innocent touch. An infant who is not held will wither and die, and psychologists have a bluntly accurate term for the failure of parents to hold and cuddle their children a great deal: abuse. And of course the special kind of community that exists between a husband and wife is given a special kind of touch.

Victorianism looked at sex and did not quite see something which is fundamentally good within a certain context. It saw something which was essentially evil (but tolerable at best within a certain context). And, in progressively widening circles, encompassing different forms of touch further and further from what is necessarily foreplay, saw that there exists at least some possibility for that touch to be sexual (at least from the perspective of the younger monk), and placed on each one a label of "This is dirty. Avoid it." Word such as "Greet one another with a kiss of love." cease to be acknowledged as a divine command which was given for human good, and instead look like, um, an odd cultural thing which, um, shows, um, um, um...

The aim, it appears, was to end up with nothing that was sexual. The result was to make everything sexual, and create a major unanticipated problem.

God created people with certain needs, and when those needs are not met, Satan comes in with counterfeit substitutes. These things are hard enough to resist to someone whose needs are met with the genuine article; when there is an immense sucking vacuum coming from unmet needs, pushing away the counterfeits acquires a difficulty which is unbelieveable. A little girl who is deprived of a father's hugs and kisses will grow into a young woman who has a tremendously difficult time avoiding sexual promiscuity, unsuccessfully searching in a series of abusive boyfriends' embraces for enough love to fill the emptiness inside.

Fortunately, most of Victorianism did not quite leave a stain that dark and deep, but there is still a major problem with a culture that refuses to wholeheartedly say, "It's OK. You may enjoy an innocent touch as an innocent touch." There is still a failure to meet a need that God created people to have filled, and still an uphill battle to fight off the counterfeit substitutes.

In this century, Victorianism has crumbled, but, like every other evil, it fails to crumble in the ways that a sane person would want it to crumble. What disappeared was not the prohibition on friendly touch, but the belief that sexual sin is a deadly poison which should be fought tooth and nail. What appeared and took the place meant to be filled by innocent touch is something which is not innocent. Thus, Victorianism did a perfect job of making room and clearing the way for a great deal of lewdness.

Current Western culture is saturated with sexual sin, not despite, but because of the fact that it is the continuation of Victorian culture.

Villain, *n.* One who is positive that his actions contribute positively to the betterment of mankind.

Among people who embody some semblance of what might be termed good, there is a continual self-search, a continual question of "Am I doing good or evil?" The Apostle Paul said, "Here is a trustworthy saying which deserves acceptance: Jesus Christ died for sinners, of whom I am the worst." Those people who act the most villainously do not ask the question, because they know that they are doing good.

Hence Nazi Germany knew that it was doing the world a favor by eradicating Jews from the face of the earth; the Jews were the source of all the world's problems. Hitler himself did not go to eradicate Jews until after he had established himself as a national hero, pulling Germany out of a major depression, and speaking love and appreciation to the common people and farmers as the heartblood of the Aryan nation. (It is the opinion of this lexicographer that, had Hitler found a more productive use for his talents than genocide, history would probably record him as a strong leader and a hero) Other groups since them, such as the Klueless Klux Klan, are also positive of the immense benefit that their actions are bringing to America, expurgating our white homeland of foreigners and helping to gently persuade them to go back to where they came from (Africa, Asia, Europe...). The present practitioners of ethnic cleansing wear watches reminding themselves of the defeat they suffered 500 years ago, and how they are merely returning just retribution and punishment to an evil that was done to them. In wartime, in order to justify the killing, it is almost universal for one nation to demonize the people of the other country and make their dominant race subhuman, entities which should be destroyed. Hence, even after the tragedy of the Viet Nam war, there was opposition to the chosen plan for a memorial because it was designed by an Asian.

Sometimes people do a more subtle job of making their actions look good. The KKK now is not openly speaking about how other races are destroying our land; they are instead speaking of the importance of hospitality and love towards whites, the true Americans. The neighbors of child molesters and mass murderers frequently say things such as, "He seemed like such a nice man."

There is one common thread; namely, that these people are masterfully adept at fighting the evil out there, and somehow never manage to look inside themselves to see if there might be evil in here.

Violence, *n.* [Lat. *violare*, also the root of 'violate'] An obsolescent term used to refer to the use of force.

> Violence is the last resort of the incompetent.
>
> -Isaac Asimov

Vote, *v.* To submit one's opinion to be counted as worthwhile.

America has a very strong tradition of overturning traditions, that is, of rejecting as inappropriate everything out of accord with the latest and most nonsensical fads. This is not a matter in which the common folk have a monopoly; among the intelligentsia, it is considered a mark of very poor taste to cite as authoritative anything not written within the past few decades. It is very much like George Orwell's novel 1984 where, when the Party changed its mind, all of the people -- lower, middle, and upper class, factory worker and scholar alike -- immediately burned down everything of the old opinion; we have a Zeitgeist instead of a Party to tell us that we should burn books, and we burn them, not by throwing them into bonfires, but by carefully keeping them in neat little rows in libraries, making them accessible, and inviting people to read them, on condition that they are not consulted for serious consideration in academic work.

Thus, it is told to people, "I don't care if you have studied years of wisdom, or are yourself a part of the years of wisdom. I don't care if you took the time to write your thoughts down in a book that has endured so that I may understand your thoughts long after your body has turned to dust. You didn't write it right now, in accordance with the present whims of the Zeitgeist, so it isn't worth my time to read."

However, America, in its own special way, does wish to keep a little of everything, not to leave a snippet of some obscure ingredient out of the great melting pot. There is thus one single place where the vote of a dead man is counted to be of equal weight to the vote of one who is alive, knowledgeable and wise in the way things should be run: Chicago.

Vulgar, *adj*. Common. The term's general usage now denotes that which is crude and distasteful. Earlier, it was used by the wealthy, the educated, and those of high social standing to refer to the habits and persons of men who are common, uneducated, and worthless, such as those whom Christ chose to be his apostles.

Vulgate, *n. Vulgate Versio*. An early translation of the Holy Scriptures, by the hand of Jerome, who wished that the Scriptures be accessible to the common man, rather than only being available in ancient language and intelligible to an elite few. See also: *AV*

Warranty, *n.* A legal document provided along with many products, in order to minimize the legal responsibility of the company which made said product to repair or replace in case of malfunction or failure to operate caused by defective workmanship. Warranty is null and void in case of damage caused by owner attempted repair, improper use, or (in some cases) normal wear.

Washington, *n.* The capital of one of the wealthiest nations in the world, and thus the location of the best government that money can buy.

Waterboarding, *n.* The fruit of a flower called the "Living Constitution" which insists that the U.S. Constitution be a dead letter.

We, *pn.* The condescending form of 'you'.

Wealth, *n.* A universally appreciated blessing which removes certain unnecessary luxuries, such as human contact.

Weapon, *n.* A powerful device enabling peace keepers to deter the occurrence of violence. The development of technology has produced weapons of increasing potency and efficiency.

> I do not know what weapons World War III will be fought with, but World War IV will be fought with sticks and stones.
>
> -Albert Einstein

Willpower, *n.* The excruciating struggle to achieve that which needs no effort.

Windows, *n.* A software emulation package used by people who cannot afford to downgrade to a slower CPU.

Wonder, *n.* Only one of many victims which has been sacrificed to the modern god, Materialism.

Word, *n.* A magnificent vessel used to convey the most profound of thoughts, and to conceal their absence.

World, *n.* The whole of fallen, unregenerate humanity, under the power of the Evil One and waging incessant warfare against the saints.

Contact with the world brings all manner of enticement to lying, idolatry, adultery, witchcraft, homosexual practice, thieving, orgies, and the like. It is rumored that there are other temptations, but they are surely not worth mentioning.

Yellow, *n.* A color symbolic of urgency and haste, used to instruct motorists to apply maximum force to the gas pedal.

Zeitgeist, *n.* The spirit of the time, made manifest in the ever more enlightened nonsensus of public opinion -- yesterday, Logical Positivism, today, Postmodernism, tomorrow, who knows? They are philosophical ideas with a kernel of truth, which has been thoughtfully removed in the popular versions. The man who follows these ideas has a mind like a steel trap -- snapped shut, and full of mice.

Zen, *adj.* and *n.*

Zenith, *n.* (1) The apex of a civilization, career, art movement, et cetera. (2) The abysmal nadir of computing.

www.ingramcontent.com/pod-product-compliance
Lightning Source LLC
Chambersburg PA
CBHW030814310726
48980CB00006B/497/J

* 9 7 8 0 6 1 5 1 9 3 6 2 5 *

"So many of us have stumbled into the ministry of administration without a mentor. How generous of Jana Holiday to provide practical wisdom for the journey! Interweaving scriptural reflection with stories from her own professional experience, Holiday identifies themes worthy of consideration by Christian administrators in a wide variety of settings."

—**Ann M. Garrido,** *Aquinas Institute of Theology*

"The gift of administration (Greek *kybernēseis,* related to the word for a ship's pilot) is what enables leaders to navigate an organization to its goal. When this gift is absent, even the best intentions are rudderless. I am profoundly grateful for Jana Holiday, whose work champions this essential contribution. Her insights don't just validate the administrator's skill set; they invest in its proper enrichment, offering a vital framework for visionaries to turn their ideas into reality."

—**Andrew Williams,** *Anglican Diocese in New England*

"In this much-needed volume, Jana Holiday has 'taken good care' to provide excellent guidance on the stewardship of administration in organizational ecosystems. Holiday creatively addresses the topic through scriptural direction, case studies, current research, and a series of very thoughtful reflection questions in each chapter. I am confident this book will be helpful to administrative leaders who are just beginning their journey as well as veterans who are looking for encouraging wisdom from a seasoned guide."

—**Donald C. Guthrie,** *Trinity Evangelical Divinity School*

"Jana Holiday turns the idea that administration is a necessary evil on its head, demonstrating how administration can be deeply formative, transformational, and indispensable for flourishing organizations. Combining rich biblical insights, theological reflections, and practical wisdom, this book is a gift to aspiring or current administrators who want to grow in their ability to take good care of organizations that they are entrusted to lead. You will come back to this book over and over again!"

—**Felix Theonugraha,** *Western Theological Seminary*